kiss

MUST LIKE KIDS

If a car could scream "no kids," his would—a slick black sports coupe with tinted windows.

Alec unfolded himself from the car, still dressed in a suit. Dark designer lenses shaded his eyes. His appearance said "important." It said, "I wield power."

He looked like anything but a fun-loving family man.

"I told you to change your clothes," she said.

"I didn't have time to stop off at my apartment."

"You might want to lose the suit coat."

"No need to say that twice."

As Alec shrugged out of it, she tried not to stare, but her gaze was pulled to the firm upper body showcased in the tailored cotton dress shirt. When her gaze returned to his face, she realized he was watching her. One side of his mouth was lifted in amusement.

Heat that had nothing to do with the broiling sun suffused her face.

Julia cleared her throat. "And the tie, too…"

DEAR READER,

Welcome to KISS! I am very excited to be writing for Harlequin's new line. I think readers are in for a real treat with these fresh-voiced, contemporary books. *Must Like Kids* marks my debut here, but I've been around for a while. In fact, I've written more than two dozen titles for Harlequin.

A little bit about my book: Poor Alec, the hero in *Must Like Kids*. He suffered through a lousy childhood, spending most of it in boarding schools or with nannies. As an adult, he's not comfortable around children. Nor does he believe himself to be the sort of man who would make a good father. He's wrong, of course. Both he and my heroine, Julia, a single mother of two, figure that out along the way.

I hope you enjoy reading their journey to happily ever after. And I hope you enjoy KISS.

As always, I welcome your comments. Drop me a note through my website at www.jackiebraun.com or find me on Facebook.

Happy reading,

Jackie Braun

MUST LIKE KIDS

———

JACKIE BRAUN

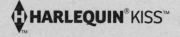

Recycling programs
for this product may
not exist in your area.

ISBN-13: 978-0-373-20707-7

MUST LIKE KIDS

HARLEQUIN®
www.Harlequin.com

ABOUT JACKIE BRAUN

———

Jackie Braun is the author of more than two dozen romance novels and novellas. She is a three-time RITA® Award finalist, a four-time National Readers' Choice Awards finalist, the winner of a Rising Star Award in traditional romantic fiction and was nominated for Series Storyteller of the Year by *RT Book Reviews* in 2008. She makes her home in mid-Michigan with her husband and their two children. She enjoys gardening and gabbing, and can be reached on Facebook or through her website at www.jackiebraun.com.

This and other titles by this author are available in ebook format—check out Harlequin.com.

For my sisters in writing at Harlequin Romance.
You all inspire me.

MUST LIKE KIDS

ONE

———

"Children have a place and it's anywhere I'm not."

Even before the reporter's eyebrows lifted, Alec McAvoy knew the words were going to come back to bite him in a place that would make sitting uncomfortable.

He laughed uneasily. "That's off the record, right?"

"This is an interview, Mr. McAvoy. Nothing is off the record," the woman interviewing him replied blandly, although he got the feeling she would be grinning broadly the first chance she got. She was young, new to her job and looking to make her mark as a journalist. He had just handed her a golden opportunity.

"Right. But you understand that I was just joking when you asked me if I liked kids? Of course I like kids. They're great. Wonderful."

Especially when they were quiet, preferably sleeping or strapped into strollers when out in public. This time he managed to keep the thoughts to himself.

"Joke or not, I find it a telling response coming from

the head of a company that specializes in products for infants and children."

To use the vernacular of the little ones to whom Best For Baby, Incorporated catered, Alec was in deep doo-doo.

No amount of backpedaling or flirting—and, yeah, he'd resorted to that before the interview was through—changed the end result. When the article hit the internet via *American CEO* magazine's online edition, it contained his flippant remark. The reporter had included his explanation that it was a "joke." Her use of quotation marks around the word only served to make it sound more insincere. But what elevated his statement from gaffe to truly damning was the reporter's inclusion of an interview she'd conducted with Alec's ex-girlfriend, Laurel McCain. No doubt Laurel had relished the chance to tarnish his reputation after their ugly breakup six months earlier. She'd wanted a ring and the title of Mrs. Alec McAvoy. He'd simply wanted out.

"Alec is uncomfortable around children," his ex claimed in the article. "We were together for nearly two years, and I can count on one hand the number of times my children were included in our outings."

No mention of the fact that she'd preferred it that way.

"Was I surprised when he was named the new head of Best For Baby back in January? Yes. Extremely," Laurel went on to say. "Don't get me wrong, Alec is a smart businessman, but as a mother, I always thought Best For Baby was about more than the bottom line."

Within hours of appearing online, the story was

picked up by a couple of high-profile bloggers. Mothers everywhere were appalled, outraged. It was shared on Facebook, tweeted about on Twitter and went viral.

Now, one week later, Alec was in the elevator at the Best For Babies headquarters in Chicago, summoned to the top floor of the thirty-story building on the banks of the Chicago River for a special meeting of the board of directors of the publicly traded company.

Deep doo-doo, indeed.

If he hadn't been apprehensive already, he would have been upon entering the conference room. A dozen, dour-faced board members were seated around the large oval of polished cherry wood. They included Herman Geller, the chairman, who steepled his fingers in front of him the way a head schoolmaster might as he waited for Alec to take a seat.

"Thank you for clearing your schedule to accommodate this special meeting today, Alec," Herman began. "We know you're a busy man, especially right now."

Alec nodded, worked up a smiled, and then, since he believed the best defense was a good offense, he launched the first volley.

"And my thanks to all of you for your time. I want to apologize again for my...verbal blunder. I understand fully the seriousness of the situation it has caused the company, and I want to assure each of you that it is being dealt with. I have our marketing department working overtime to reach out to our customers and reassure them that Best For Baby is not a hard-hearted company that is solely profit-driven. We're calling the campaign 'One Big Family' and focusing on how the

Best For Baby family is with our customers' families every step of the way."

"Yes, I received your memorandum on that a couple of days ago. I especially like the idea of including photographs of our workers' children." But the older man didn't appear satisfied. He tugged at one unruly eyebrow before saying, "At this point, Alec, it's not only the consumer who needs to be reassured. Our investors do, too."

Alec nodded and reached for the glass of ice water that was already poured and waiting on the table in front of him. His throat felt parched. It remained that way even after he took a sip.

"Like all of you, I am very disappointed with the drop in our stock's value." Some media outlets were using words such as *tanking* and *free-fall* to describe the double-digit plummet the stock had taken in a matter of days. "I've drafted a letter to shareholders that should allay their concerns." He swiped a finger over the condensation forming on the outside of the glass. Forget parched. His throat felt scorched now as he pushed out the rest of the words. "In addition to my personal apology, I am willing to tender my resignation if our stock has not rebounded within the next three months."

"That's commendable, Alec," Herman replied. "Let's hope it won't come to that. We would hate to lose someone of your caliber over a publicity debacle such as this."

Reading between the lines, Alec knew they would, though. They would shake him off even sooner if need be. Still, it appeared that his employment wasn't on the agenda of today's meeting. Alec was just starting to relax when the older man said, "That's why, in a special meeting of the board yesterday, it was decided that we would bring in a consultant to help us with damage control."

The board had convened two special meetings in as many days? And the first one had been conducted without his knowledge. That didn't bode well.

"A consultant?" he asked, embarrassed to hear his voice crack.

"Yes. She comes highly recommended and is eager to get started."

Alec blinked at that. "You've already been in contact with her?"

Which meant today's special meeting wasn't to ask his opinion, but to render the board's verdict. He didn't like being left out of the loop.

"Under the circumstances, we thought it best to act quickly. Our stockholders are demanding action."

Dexter Roth from marketing was going to be irked, Alec thought. Same for Franklin Kirby, their advertising representative. Alec had asked the two men to head up the multipronged media blitz set to be unveiled this coming weekend. They were not going to be happy that an outside consultant was being brought in as the point person. Alec said as much now.

"Julia Stillwell will be part of the One Big Family campaign, an integral part," Herman said. "She's an image consultant."

Alec's brows hiked up. "An image..."

"Consultant," Herman finished for him. His gaze was unflinching, although no one else around the table would meet Alec's eye. "For better or worse, you are the face of this company. The public needs to get to know you better. They need to like you, trust you. They need to know that even though you are a bachelor with no children of your own, you aren't antifamily or antichild."

"I'm not."

Just because he wasn't interested in having a wife and kids didn't mean he had anything against either marriage or parenthood. Some men were hardwired for the roles of husband and father. Alec—the product of a pair of freewheeling, free-spending parents, who had packed him off to boarding school so they could continue their jet-setting, hard-partying ways— figured he wasn't. No way would he put another kid through the emotionally sterile childhood he'd endured, spending holidays and summers with nannies and other adults who'd been paid to watch over him.

"Excellent." Herman glanced at his watch. "Your first meeting with her will be in less than an hour. She has a full schedule today, but has graciously agreed to fit you in."

"How lucky for me," he managed to say and forced a smile in case his sarcasm came through.

"You'll need to go to her office, though. I've given your secretary the address. Ms. Stillwell asked that you be on time. She has a pressing appointment immediately after yours."

"I'd better head out now, then."

Alec pushed back his chair and rose. Irritation had replaced the apprehension he'd experienced upon entering the room. An image consultant! The idea was galling.

Herman's parting words of "good luck" did little to improve his mood.

Julia Stillwell checked her watch against the clock on the wall. Alec McAvoy had one minute and forty-eight seconds to be at her door for their thirty-minute appointment. Punctuality was rule number one in her book. When people were late it said they didn't think other people's time was as valuable as their own. It also wreaked havoc on her ridiculously tight personal timetable.

As a single mother with two young children, she knew only too well the importance of staying on schedule. If she was late leaving the office, it meant she would be late picking up her kids from school, which in turn meant Danielle would be late for dance class or Colin for T-ball, or whatever else was on tap for that day. As it was, being a parent made life unpredictable, an adventure. She tried to see that as a plus, but on days such as this, she wasn't always successful.

She'd been up since 4:00 a.m., jolted from sleep by a put-out Danielle. The nine-year-old had been none too happy to have to share her bed with her six-year-old brother, Colin, who'd climbed in with her after having a bad dream. Julia had checked under his bed and in his closet for the green-goo-oozing monster of his nightmare. Even after giving him the all clear, he'd been unable to fall back to sleep in his own room. So, all three of them had wound up in her full-sized bed, where none had managed another wink.

Julia fought back a yawn now as she glanced at the clock again. Alec McAvoy was officially late. When he arrived, assuming he did before she had to leave, she would offer him a cup of coffee so she could have some herself. One thing she wouldn't be doing, however, was adding any time onto the end of the appointment to accommodate him. It might be his money, or more accurately Best For Baby's, but it was her time. And she had better things to do with it—such as ensure Colin got to his T-ball game on time.

A high-powered executive such as Mr. McAvoy probably wouldn't or couldn't appreciate that. Julia didn't stop to wonder if she might be judging him too harshly. After all, she'd been hired to rescue him from the deep hole he'd dug for himself, one that was costing his company and its investors millions of dollars, all because of an inflammatory statement. Slip of the tongue? Perhaps. But she didn't buy for a minute that he'd intended the comment as a joke.

Professionally and in her personal life, Julia had met a lot of men like Alec. Men who viewed family obligations, children in particular, as an inconvenience, a burden. It was why, in the four years since her husband's death, she'd only gone on a handful of dates. Men were interested in getting to know her until they learned that she came with a side order of kids. Then Julia found herself off the menu. It was their loss.

It was Alec McAvoy's loss, too, she thought, glancing at the folder marked with his name.

She propped a hip on the edge of her desk, picked up the file and leafed through it again as she waited with growing impatience for him to arrive. The photograph was the one that had accompanied the story. It showed a handsome man in his mid-thirties clad in an expertly tailored charcoal suit, dark blue shirt and conservative-print silk tie. A handkerchief of the same print and fabric as the tie peeked from his breast pocket.

"I bet you've never wiped a runny nose with that," she mused aloud.

Julia exhaled slowly. She had to convince mothers the country over that this bachelor CEO of a company that catered to children wasn't antikid. The task wouldn't be easy, especially if she didn't put her heart into it. She didn't have to like him, she reminded herself. But she had to make sure everyone else did. Still, it would help if she liked him. If she found his personality as appealing as his dark eyes and sexy smile. She frowned and glanced at her watch again. Unfortunately, there wasn't much to like about a man who kept her waiting when she'd gone to the trouble of rescheduling another appointment to fit him in.

Fifteen minutes later, her foot was tapping in agitation when a knock sounded at the door. Sandy, her assistant, poked her head into the room, her expression apprehensive. The young woman knew Julia's feelings about tardiness, having been on the receiving end of a lecture more than once when she'd first started.

"Mr. McAvoy is here. Shall I show him in or do you want me to reschedule his appointment for another day?"

As tempting as it was to go with the latter, Julia had made a commitment to the Best For Baby board, so she said, "I'll see him now, thanks. I have a few minutes to spare before I have to leave."

She ordered herself to be welcoming and enthusiastic. If the image makeover she planned to give him failed to turn around public opinion, she didn't want it to be because of anything she hadn't done. It would be all his doing, she decided, when Alec strode into her office with an obvious chip weighting his shoulder. He didn't want to be here. More than that, he resented being forced to come. The grim set of his jaw made that much clear.

She pegged him as the take-charge sort. That type didn't like being told what to do, regardless of the reason. Still, Julia hoped she wasn't going to have to waste precious time trying to convince him they were playing on the same team.

In person, he was taller than she'd expected him to be, surpassing the six-foot mark by at least a couple of inches. His shoulders were broader than she'd guessed from the photo, and she could see now that it was the result of actual muscle rather than a tailor's creative needlework. As she studied him, an inappropriate amount of awareness stirred in her, the likes of which she hadn't experienced in a very long time. At her sharp intake of breath, the dark brows over his glass-bottle-green eyes rose fractionally.

He appeared caught off guard as well. For the briefest of moments, feminine vanity had her hoping it was for the same reason she'd been taken aback: attraction—both potent and instantaneous. She dismissed the thought. She was being ridiculous, foolish, which wasn't like her. More likely, he was surprised by her appearance. A lot of people were when they met her. Julia looked harmless rather than high-powered, as if she should be teaching Sunday school or volunteering for the PTO—both of which she did—rather than single-handedly manipulating the media and realigning the public's mindset. A client once told her that was her advantage. She certainly used it as one.

Sure enough, he said, "*You're* Miss Stillwell?"

"Actually, I go by Ms."

"Ms." He nodded, and she thought she heard a hint of derision in his tone when he added, "Of course."

He extended a hand. It was big and warm, and it nearly swallowed up the one that she offered to him in return.

"Why don't you have a seat, Mr. McAvoy." She gestured toward a chair. Perhaps sitting he wouldn't appear quite as imposing.

He shook his head. "This won't do."

Uh-oh. "Excuse me?"

She girded for an argument, but it turned out the effort was unwarranted.

"The courtesy titles. Can we drop them? They make me feel like I'm back in boarding school."

Boarding school. Which meant he'd grown up in privilege and was used to having far more than his basic needs met. She narrowed in on another clue to his personality. "Let me guess. You had a problem with authority in those days."

"Sometimes." She caught a glimmer of rebellion in his green eyes. "Rules are made to be broken."

"Not my rules. And punctuality is one of them," she told him pointedly.

"I suppose you're expecting an apology for my being late."

"Now that you mention it, that wouldn't be a bad place to start."

"Sorry." His mouth curved into a smile.

Julia ignored the effect it had on her pulse and instead folded her arms. "Is that the best you can do? No wonder your board of directors hired me."

That had his smile flattening into a tight line.

"I can be persuasive when I want to be." His gaze shifted south briefly, leaving her to feel exposed even though she knew her neckline to be modest. Then he offered a smile that would have been right at home in the bedroom during foreplay.

Julia wanted to be insulted or outraged or, at the very least, irritated. What she felt was aroused…awakened. That feeling did make her irritated—with both of them.

"Let's get another one of my rules clear. I have nothing against flattery. In fact, I find that it comes in handy in my line of work. But I am immune to it. You're not here as my date. You're here as my client. Save the smoldering looks for your girlfriend."

His brows rose again. "That was direct."

"I don't believe in beating around the bush or playing games. What would be the point? Games are for children."

"Yes, and apparently I need help where they are concerned, at least in terms of my public image." His lips returned to a grim line.

"You don't want to be here," she remarked.

"No, I don't, but I wasn't given a choice."

She wasn't the only one who believed in being direct, apparently.

"You made a mess, Mr....Alec."

"A big one," he agreed. "But I prefer to clean up after myself."

"A man who likes to clean up after himself." She pursed her lips in mock consideration. "As pleasing as I find that attribute in a member of the opposite sex, I've been hired to do a job, namely to save yours and pull your company's stock out of the basement. So, we can be adversaries or you can help me help you."

He was quiet a moment. Finally, after exhaling deeply, he asked, "What will all this entail?"

Julia had had less than twenty-four hours to work on a plan, but she didn't mention that. Besides, he'd talked to the board of directors, so he knew. If he was expecting excuses, he wouldn't get them from her.

"Have a seat." She motioned again to one of the chairs angled in front of her desk and returned to where she'd been, with one hip on the edge, preferring the height advantage it gave her. He had to look up to her now. "In addition to rebutting the information provided in the original article—"

"That's been done," he interrupted.

"Not by me, it hasn't." Julia had read the follow-up article. She'd probably been in the minority there. His response to the original article certainly hadn't gone viral. "As I was saying, in addition to my rebuttal and some well-placed stories in other media outlets, both traditional and digital, we need to find, or if need be, manufacture, as many opportunities as possible in the coming weeks for you to be photographed and filmed with children."

His eyes narrowed. "What children?"

"I don't suppose you are close to any? Nephews? Nieces?" she asked. Thanks to her older sister, Eloise, Julia had one of each. It would be great if Alec had an actual relationship with the little ones who would be used in the photo opportunities she had planned. When her question was met with stony silence, she added, "Leave that to me."

"You used the word *manufacture*."

"We can't expect invitations to such events to fall into our laps in a timely fashion. That's why I propose Best For Baby hold some kind of community event here in Chicago to start and perhaps locations elsewhere around the country if I feel that's necessary. It will coincide with your One Big Family campaign."

"So, what? You're going to have me kissing babies like a politician on the campaign trail?" He looked more appalled than amused.

"If need be. Do you have a problem with that?" She wanted to know right then how much of a battle she was in for.

A muscle ticked in his jaw. "I'll reserve judgment."

Julia straightened and went behind her desk, where she picked up a spreadsheet. Handing it to Alec, she said, "These are some of the events I have in mind. The two highlighted in green have been confirmed." They'd been easy to pin down, since the organizers had been desperate for corporate sponsorship, which is what they'd been promised in return. "The ones in yellow are tentative. There will be more, but this is a start."

He barely spared the paper a glance before saying, "I'll check my schedule and get back to you."

"Actually, you'll *clear* your schedule, and *I'll* get back to *you* with talking points and suggested attire."

"You're going to pick out my clothing?" He rose to his feet. He didn't look happy at the prospect. A lot of clients, especially those who came to her under duress, didn't like being told how to dress. She couldn't blame them, but that didn't change anything.

"You can wear whatever you want to the office or on your own time," she told him. "But for these events, yes, I'll be picking out your clothes. What you wear needs to help convey the message we want to send."

"What messages are my clothes sending?"

She glanced down and swallowed an inappropriate sigh. She managed to sound completely professional when she replied, "They tell me you take a great deal of care with your appearance and that you have the means to buy what you want, regardless of the price tag."

"And that's bad?"

"Most of the people buying Best For Baby's products can't relate to your lifestyle, Alec."

He folded his arms over his chest. "Are you calling me a snob?"

"I'm not calling you anything."

"But that's what you think?"

"What I think isn't the issue here. That's the signal you will send if we're not careful. It's all about image."

She braced for further argument, but he said, "You're the expert."

"Yes, I am."

Julia wasn't fooled by his easy capitulation. She and

Alec McAvoy were going to butt heads a lot before their association ended. In a perverse way, she was looking forward to it.

TWO

—

    It was like playing a chess match, Alec thought. Or maybe a game of blink, waiting for the other person to close their eyes first. It was a bit galling when he was the one who did.

Julia Stillwell was a surprise. And not just because she was five and half feet of tidy curves tucked into a creamy silk blouse and conservative navy pencil skirt. She was pretty, nonthreatening. The girl next door. She disarmed her opponents with a cherubic smile, dimples included, that took one's mind off her waspish sting. But the real kicker was the unsettling amount of attraction he felt for her. It had landed like a prize-fighter's punch to the midsection the moment he'd walked through her door. He was still struggling to regain his footing.

Fifteen minutes into their meeting, she glanced at her watch—though he didn't doubt for a moment that she already knew the exact time—and said, "I have to be going, but I'll be in touch tomorrow morning."

"Hot date?" he asked, just to see if he could rile her.

No one should be that composed. And, okay, he was curious, too.

She didn't look the least bit ruffled. In fact, the smile she sent him was relaxed and filled with humor. "Of a fashion."

What in the heck did that mean?

A couple of pictures were propped on her desk, but from his position, Alec couldn't make out their subject matter. Were they of her husband? No. He hadn't noticed a ring on her finger, and he'd made a point of looking. A lover, then?

Irked by his own curiosity more than by her evasive response, Alec said, "Isn't it a little early to be knocking off for the day. It's not even five o'clock."

Still standing, she bent and logged off the computer, but not before clicking on a file. On the credenza behind her, the printer fired to life and began spitting out pages.

As she turned around to collect them, she asked, "How late do you work?"

"Until six at least, seven on occasion." In truth, he'd been known to stay past eight and was on a first-name basis with his building's cleaning crew and the night security detail.

"For a total of how many hours a week?"

"Usually fifty to sixty." Or, as had been the case the previous week, seventy-five.

She shook her head. Her expression said, *I thought so.*

"Well, I put in forty hours at my office. Never more than forty. I start my day early so that I can be out of here early." She glanced at her watch again. "In fact, today I've stayed five minutes late. To accommodate you."

She tapped the papers she'd gathered into a neat pile and reached for the stapler. Her efficient movements were the perfect complement to her words.

"Don't you ever clock some overtime? I would think, given the urgency of my situation and what you are being paid to address it, that you would be happy to log a few extra hours here and there."

He'd hoped that would get a rise out of her, but he wasn't successful. Not completely, anyway, although he did detect a slight edge to her tone when she told him, "I believe in balance. I have a life. In fact, my personal life has been known to take precedence over pulling in a paycheck when that's what I feel is warranted."

"The perk of being your own boss?"

"That's right. I made a decision a long time ago that my children would come first."

"You have children?" he blurted out, immediately aware of how the question came across. Sure enough, Julia's expression tightened.

"Two, but don't worry. They've had all their shots." She turned the photographs on her desk around. A pair of elementary school-age kids smiled back, one of each sex, both sporting their mother's deep dimples.

"Sorry." He rubbed a hand over the back of his neck.

She nodded. "You've had to do a lot of apologizing lately where children are concerned."

"I've got nothing against kids." God help him. He was starting to sound like a broken record.

She nodded again. "Here's a tip. Free of charge. My job here is what I do. It's not who I am, which is why I choose not to spend every waking hour at it. There's more to life than work, Alec."

"You sound like my mother."

"I'll take that as a compliment," Julia replied.

He hadn't intended it as one. Her wry expression told him she suspected as much. Alec's parents lived extravagantly and well beyond their means. Even before he had graduated from college, they had burned through his mother's substantial inheritance. If not for his paternal grandfather's interference, they would have wound up homeless and penniless, and Alec would have been forced to drop out of his Ivy League school before receiving his degree.

Granddad was gone now, but before he'd died he'd made sure to put the money he left in a trust, one that Alec administered. As such, his parents had to come to him for everything. Neither party was particularly happy about it.

Indeed, that was why Alec had arrived late to his appointment with Julia. Just prior to leaving his office, his mother had phoned him in a panic. Even though they were only a week into June, she and Alec's father needed more money. They'd used up their generous monthly stipend to purchase airline tickets—first class, of course—and book a two-week stay with friends at an exclusive resort on a small, private island in the Caribbean. They didn't leave for another week and now they had nothing left to buy groceries. Nor did they have any spending money for their trip.

He'd put down his foot. Or he'd tried to. Finally, to get his crying mother off the phone, Alec had agreed to transfer an additional seven grand into his parents' bank account. He'd held firm on the amount, even when she'd insisted they needed at least ten thousand.

"Be reasonable, Alec. How can your father and I have a proper vacation with so little to spend?" she'd demanded.

"Order a glass of wine with dinner instead of a magnum of champagne," he'd suggested. "And don't buy a round of drinks for the entire nightclub."

"You're such a stick in the mud, Alec. All you do is work. You don't know how to have fun," Brooke had sighed before relenting and hanging up.

His parents would have their vacation, and he would have a little peace and quiet—a reprieve of sorts until the next phone call reporting a crisis. And there would be another one, Alec knew. They came as regularly as gusts of wind in Chicago.

Thinking of the conversation now, he assured Julia, "I know how to enjoy myself away from the office."

"Yes. That came through in the article," Julia replied dryly. "Your ex-girlfriend mentioned that the pair of you enjoyed first-class travel, fine dining, golf."

"Is there something wrong with that?" He might not take vacations as often as his parents or for as long as they did, but when he took one, he enjoyed himself.

The corners of her mouth turned down in consideration. Julia had nice lips. Soft. Full. They were one of her most inviting facial features...even when she was frowning at him. "On the surface, not a thing. Except that her children weren't involved."

His voice rose and, despite his best efforts, his tone turned defensive. "Laurel didn't *want* them involved. That was her call. It was her decision."

At nine and eleven, Laurel's two daughters were miniature versions of their mother, and as such, extremely high-maintenance, which was why Laurel preferred to leave them to their nanny.

"Did you ever try to change her mind?"

"Does it matter?" he asked.

"To me? No. To the public, it would, yes."

He exhaled in frustration now. "Look, I've never claimed to be a family man. I'm a businessman. A damned good one, in fact, which is why Best For Baby brought me on board. The company needed a qualified executive. My personal life shouldn't be an issue."

"It wouldn't be if you hadn't opened your mouth and made it one," Julia shot back without missing a beat. "Which brings us back to square one, Alec."

He cursed and returned to his seat. He hated that she was right. As he scrubbed a hand down his face, Julia was saying, "You can't change what you said. It's on the record and will be winging around cyberspace indefinitely. What we can change is your image going forward."

"I know." His hand fell away, but it curled into a fist at his side, mirroring the position of the left one.

"Good." She continued to drive home the point. Her tone became instructional, perhaps to offset the censure inherent in her words. "To the baby-product-buying public, you are the epitome of a playboy. You have the position and enough power and wealth to subsidize a very adult lifestyle. It doesn't hurt that you grew up in privilege."

He snorted at that. Sometimes privilege was just another word for lonely.

She was saying, "Golf, fine dining, first-class travel at all-inclusive resorts not known for their child-friendly amenities—these are very adult activities. As such, they aren't going to help us convince the broader public that you understand family life or its particular needs."

"So you're going to have me be seen out and about in public, kissing babies. Got it." He sighed and made his hands unclench.

"That's not exactly the attitude I'm hoping you'll project."

"I'll work on it," he grumbled.

She made a humming noise. Then her gaze narrowed. "How about a test run this evening?"

He frowned. "I'm not following you."

"What do you have on your schedule for six o'clock?"

He did a mental check of his calendar. "A meeting with the head of the accounting department at five to go over some expense report irregularities. I don't know if it will be concluded by then."

"Really? A meeting after regular business hours? You can't be a very popular boss." She shook her head, forestalling his reply. "Can you reschedule it?"

"I guess so," he said slowly. "Why?"

Those full lips bloomed into a smile that managed to be sexy despite the calculating gleam in her eyes. "Have you ever been to a T-ball game?"

What was she thinking, inviting Alec to join her at the game?

Julia asked herself the question a dozen times as she maneuvered through traffic after picking up her children from St. Augustine's after-school program. Her goal was that Danielle and Colin never had to spend more than two hours there on any given day. Except during the summer. In another week, the school year would wrap up, and her children would be spending three days a week there, with the other two at their grandparents' just outside the city.

Guilt nipped, as it always did, even though it couldn't be helped. She was a working mother, the sole breadwinner. The after-school program wasn't a bad one. The kids went on field trips to places such as Chicago's Field Museum of Natural History, Navy Pier and the John C. Shedd Aquarium. But before they were born, Julia had pictured their lives differently. She'd planned to be a stay-at-home mom. For a brief time she had been. Then Scott had gotten sick and plans had changed.

"What's for dinner?" Colin asked from the backseat as she brought the car to a stop at a light.

"Turkey grinders from Howard's Deli," Julia replied, deciding not to add that they would be on whole wheat buns with slices of tomato and green peppers and shredded lettuce to at least make them a somewhat balanced meal.

In the rearview mirror, she watched his face scrunch up. "Can't it be cheeseburgers? Please, please, please!"

Danielle sighed, and in a superior tone, said, "He only wants the toy that comes with the children's meal."

She was nine, going on nineteen. It scared Julia sometimes, how serious and mature her daughter could be.

"You've got that line between your eyebrows, Mommy," Colin observed. "Does that mean you're thinking about it?"

To ward off further argument, Julia said, "Maybe."

A snort sounded from the backseat. "When parents say they're thinking about something or use the word *maybe,* it means no," Danielle said. "Mom has been *thinking* about letting me go to art camp for a month now."

Julia caught a glimpse of her daughter's mutinous expression. "I *am* thinking about it. I haven't ruled it out, Danielle."

Where the camp was located and how much it cost weren't what caused Julia's stomach to drop. A full week away? Could Danielle handle that? Could Julia?

"I really want to go," her daughter said quietly.

"I want to go, too!" Colin shouted. "Can I go, too, Mommy?"

"You can't," Danielle insisted. "It's not for babies. Besides, you can't even color inside the lines!"

Colin sent up a wail that rivaled a fire truck's siren. By the time they reached the baseball diamond fifty-five minutes and one stop at the deli later, Julia had a raging headache. She barely had a chance to shift the car into Park before Colin was unbuckled and out the door.

"Hey! Come back and get your bag!" she called after him before he could get too far.

Julia had enough to tote, what with lawn chairs and a portable canopy that she kept on hand to shield them from the blazing afternoon sun. Danielle was of little help since she was carrying the bottles of water they'd picked up at the deli.

As Julia slammed the trunk closed, a slick, black sports coupe with tinted windows pulled into the parking space next to hers. It came as no surprise when Alec unfolded himself from the driver's side of the foreign-made two-seater. If a car could scream "no kids," this one would.

He was still dressed in a suit, although he'd thought to loosen his tie. Mirrored, designer lenses shaded his eyes. His appearance said important. It said, *I wield power.* He looked like anything but a fun-loving family man.

"I've got my work cut out for me," Julia muttered and forced a smile.

It didn't help that the first words out of his mouth were a complaint. "It's broiling out here."

"Be thankful we're the home team today. Fans of the visiting team will be looking straight into the sun for the entire game."

"Is that supposed to make me feel better?"

She shrugged. "I told you to change your clothes."

She had, happily trading in heels and a skirt for shorts and flat sandals when they'd grabbed dinner at the deli. "This is T-ball."

"I didn't have time to stop off at my apartment if I wanted make it here on time. Our meeting earlier aside, I do try to be punctual."

She nodded her acceptance of what she figured he intended as an apology. "You might want to lose the suit coat."

"No need to say that twice."

As Alec shrugged out of it, she tried not to stare, but her gaze was pulled to the firm upper body showcased in the tailored cotton dress shirt. Genetics alone weren't responsible for those shoulders or that chest. He might spend a lot of hours behind a desk, but he made time for exercise. When her gaze returned to his face, she realized he was watching her. One side of his mouth was lifted in amusement. Heat that had nothing to do with the soaring mercury suffused her face.

She cleared her throat. "The tie, too," she added after he carefully laid the jacket over his car's seat.

"You're the expert."

He freed the tie with a gentle tug. Even though they were out in public, the gesture came across as intimate.

What was she thinking?

This time, the question Julia posed to herself had nothing to do with her spontaneous invitation to the T-ball game and everything to do with feminine awareness. Hormones she'd forgotten she had, started to sizzle and snap to life. It was ridiculous. It was a relief, a small voice whispered. Flustered, Julia glanced away, only to have her gaze land on Danielle, who was watching her, too.

"Who is this?" her daughter demanded bluntly.

Julia would have a word with her later about her manners. For now she said, "This is Mr. McAvoy. He's a client. Alec, these are my children, Danielle and Colin."

Danielle was undeterred. "Why is he here?"

"Isn't that obvious?" Colin said. "He wants to watch my game."

"That's right, champ." Alec touched the brim of her son's cap. The gesture came off as choreographed and his words sounded overly enthusiastic. While Julia gave him points for trying, his awkwardness around kids came through loud and clear.

Danielle rolled her eyes.

"We're not champs." Colin lowered his squeaky voice to a confidential whisper. "Just so you know, for T-ball, they don't even keep score."

"Oh." Alec glanced over at Julia, his expression not so much sheepish as unnerved. No doubt about it. He was operating outside his comfort zone.

"Why is he here, Mom?" Danielle demanded again.

"Danielle," Julia replied in a tone that was stern despite being soft. She sent an apologetic smile in Alec's direction.

"It's all right."

It wasn't, but Julia told her daughter, "Mr. McAvoy doesn't have children, but he needs to know a little bit more about them for his job. So, I have agreed to help him."

"You're not dating, though. Right?"

"No!"

"Good." What was that supposed to mean? Danielle didn't give Julia much of a chance to wonder, before adding, "So, we're guinea pigs?"

"Actually, I think I'm the guinea pig," Alec replied.

Danielle's brows drew together in consideration. "Kids are a lot of work, you know."

"So I've been told."

"Think you're up to it?" she asked baldly. "Most single men aren't."

He glanced over at Julia, who smiled weakly. She'd

never said as much out loud, but she was left to wonder if that was the message she'd been telegraphing.

"I hope so," he answered. "My job is sort of depend-
ing on it."

"You came to the right person," Colin assured him
with a gap-toothed grin. "Our mom knows everything."

Alec wasn't much for know-it-alls, but when they
looked like Julia Stillwell, he was willing to make an
exception, especially if her efforts succeeded in turning around his public image and professional future.

He had to admit, her kids seemed bright and well-
adjusted...if a little outspoken in the daughter's case.
The apple hadn't fallen far from the tree apparently.
It was clear Julia loved them and, just as importantly,
put them first. That was something his ex-girlfriend
hadn't done. Something his parents had never managed. The fact that she kicked off early on a regular
basis and was willing to sit outside in the broiling sun
at a T-ball game was proof of that. He couldn't help
wondering, what had happened to Mr. Stillwell?

The kids tumbled on ahead, Colin hoisting his
equipment bag, Danielle carrying the water bottles.

Alec remembered his manners then.

"Can I carry something?"

"You can. Thanks." Julia handed over a portable
canopy. It folded up into a duffel bag that measured
nearly four feet long. Alec frowned as he hefted it to
his shoulder.

"This is heavy."

"You can take the chairs, if you'd prefer."

He bristled a little at that. "I'm not complaining.

I'm just surprised you were able to carry this." He nodded to the chairs and her oversized purse. "And all that, too."

"I'm a mom. We tote stuff around all the time." She didn't appear insulted as much as amused.

And sexy. Yeah, definitely sexy, with her sleek arms loaded in such a way that the strain caused her cotton T-shirt to pull across her breasts.

"Do I look frail?" she asked.

"You look...fit." It wasn't what he planned to say, but Alec figured the first adjective that had popped to mind might get him smacked.

They made their way to the diamond. Three small trees were staggered behind the home team's bench. Every square inch of the meager shade they provided was occupied with people on blankets or seated in folding chairs.

"You've got to get here early to score a spot in the shade," she said, noting the direction of his gaze. She nodded to the duffel bag he carried. "That's why I bring my own. I learned that lesson the hard way the first year Danielle played."

Her daughter had stopped to talk to a couple of girls who looked to be about her age.

"Does she still play?" Alec asked. She was a cute little thing despite her penchant for speaking her mind.

"T-ball? Not anymore. Too old. She played one year of coach-pitch baseball, but now she's into soccer. She has a game on Saturday."

"Are you telling me I need to clear my schedule again?" he teased.

Julia's tone was thoughtful. "We'll see. You might

need another dry run, so to speak, before I turn you loose on kids who are more impressionable than mine."

It was an interesting assessment. Alec wanted to be insulted, but before he could express any indignation, Julia was calling for her son to stop playing in the chalky dirt next to the home team's bench. A couple of the other kids were doing the same thing, and their parents were after them too as soon as a stifling breeze kicked up and began carrying the dust out toward the spectators.

"Serious ballplayers, I see."

The kids all wore bright orange jerseys and ball caps, sporting the sponsor's name. If they were bothered by the heat or the now gritty air, they didn't show it.

Julia laughed. The sound was pleasant, as was the way humor lit up her eyes and caused the dimples to dent her cheeks.

"Wait till they let ground balls slip by in the outfield because they're too busy picking dandelions, or the game has to be stopped for a few minutes because the batter has lost a tooth." She stopped walking and set down the chairs. "This is a good spot."

Five minutes and one pinched finger later, the canopy was up and they were ensconced in a pair of relatively comfortable lawn chairs underneath it. Out of the sun, the heat was almost tolerable.

"How's your finger?" she inquired politely. She'd been scanning the area, waving to this person and calling out a greeting to that one. All the while, she kept an eye on her kids.

Alec studied the purplish welt just between the first and second knuckles on his index finger. "No worse than my pride. How do you get this thing up by your-self?"

"I don't. Colin and Danielle are too small to be much help, but I can usually recruit another parent or two to give me a hand."

As if on cue, a large woman wearing a baseball cap and a shirt emblazoned with Logan's Mom ambled into view.

"Hey, Julia, I was just making my way over to help when I saw you didn't need me. So, who's your new friend?"

She grinned at Alec, openly curious. He'd already noticed some of the parents casting furtive glances his way. Julia was going to have some explaining to do at the next game, he figured, amused.

"This is Alec McAvoy. He's a...business associate. Alec, this is Karen Croswell. She's—"

"Logan's mom," he finished for her.

Karen glanced down at her well-endowed chest. Her son's name began to jiggle with her accompanying laughter. When her gaze returned to Alec's it held as much feminine interest as it did humor.

"So, you and Julia know one another through work, hmm?"

"That's right."

Julia cleared her throat. "Alec is a client. I invited him along so he could get a feel for what parents go through."

The explanation filled in some blanks while also being cryptic enough to raise more questions.

"Oh? Are you and your wife expecting a child?"

He decided it was easier just to play along with her fishing expedition. "No kids, no wife."

Although it was true, he didn't appreciate the way Julia added, "Alec is married to his career."

If she'd been trying to warn off Karen, it backfired. "So you're *just* a client of Julia's."

"Right."

"Yep. That's all," Julia agreed.

Karen's eyes lit up like twin Christmas trees. "Like Julia, here, I'm a single mom. That's why the two of us stick together at T-ball games. We help each other out with things like raising canopies. The other moms have husbands to give them a hand."

He glanced at Julia. Her expression was inscrutable. "Julia looks like she manages just fine. She's—"

"Fit," Julia finished for him. "Or so I've been told."

"I meant it as a compliment."

"And I took it as one."

Alec wondered.

Karen, who'd been watching their exchange, was frowning. Confused no doubt. He couldn't say he blamed her.

She said, "Julia is a lot more resourceful than I am. I don't know what I'd do without her."

"You'd be fine, Karen," Julia replied with a patient smile. Then added, "Are Logan's allergies flaring up again? He looks like he could use a tissue before the game starts."

Karen withdrew, but not before shaking Alec's hand again. "It was really nice to meet you. Maybe I'll see you again. I'd be happy to help you research what parents go through."

"I'll keep that in mind."

"Karen comes on a little...strong, but she has a good heart," Julia remarked when they were alone again.

"She seemed...nice." He didn't know what else to say.

"She's not your type, I gather."

"No." He said it slowly, mentally glancing around for land mines.

"Kids can be a turnoff."

Uh-oh. "My interest or lack thereof in this case has nothing to do with her being a single mother."

"Oh, that's right. You'll date women with children, as long as nannies are involved."

Forget land mines. It was his temper that was threatening to blow now. Alec counted to ten. Even then his tone was sharp. "That's not fair."

She shrugged, unbothered by either his tone or his assertion. "That's how you come across to the baby-product-buying public."

Only the baby-product-buying public? he wondered. But he said, "As I already told you, I didn't have anything against Laurel's children, and they certainly weren't the reason things between us ended." At Julia's raised brows, he added, "The relationship simply ran its course."

Julia nodded. But did she believe him? And why did he care if she did?

"Are you seeing anyone now?" she surprised him by asking.

"That's a little personal, don't you think?"

"Personal, but relevant. So, are you?"

"No. I'm between relationships." He waited a beat, then asked, "What about you?"

"That's both personal *and* irrelevant."

Alec ground his molars together. God, the woman was exasperating. And he had to work with her for who knew how long. It was just his luck.

"Let's get back to your friend Karen. As I said, she seems nice enough, but I'm not interested. Attraction is hard to quantify." His instantaneous attraction to the prickly woman seated beside him being a case in point. "I date women I find engaging, exciting."

"And deep, no doubt."

Julia's lips twitched, leaving him with the impression she was laughing at him.

"You think I'm shallow?"

She sobered at that and glanced away. "I'm sorry. That was rude. I'm not being paid to pass judgments."

Her answer was hardly reassuring. She pointed in the direction her friend had gone.

"For the record, Karen's ex is a total deadbeat. Gordie hasn't seen Logan or their girls in more than a year, nor has he paid child support. If not for Karen's parents, Logan wouldn't have a roof over his head, much less be playing T-ball. So, she tends to come on a little strong when she realizes a man is both unmarried and gainfully employed."

Bitterness welled in Alec's throat as he recalled his own childhood. Even parents who stayed married could be deadbeats, he thought.

"You'll have to work on that," Julia remarked. Her tone was clipped.

"What?"

"That look of supreme distaste. She's not a gold digger. She's just looking for companionship and a father figure for her kids."

He didn't bother trying to correct Julia's assumption that he'd been thinking about Karen. The last thing he wanted to talk about was his parents. Instead, he decided to shift the focus of their conversation. "What about you? You're a single mom, too. Are you looking for those things?"

She shook her head. Despite the heat, her tone was pure frost when she replied, "My kids and I are fine on our own."

THREE

The game ended. The crowd dispersed. Alec helped Julia take down the canopy and carry it back to her car.

"I'll be in touch," she said.

He nodded. "Nice meeting you," he said to her kids, adding, "Good game," for Colin's benefit.

"We got creamed."

Alec frowned. "I thought you said no one keeps score."

"The coaches don't, but Noah Wilson's dad does. He said it was a massacre, and we need to work on our catching."

"Oh."

"There's one of those dads on every team," Julia muttered.

"Do you know much about baseball?" Colin asked. "Maybe we could play catch some time."

"Um..." Alec's gaze cut to her.

Julia knew panic when she saw it. "Mr. McAvoy is a busy man, Colin."

Colin nodded at the explanation. "Oh. Okay." To Alec he said, "That's too bad. Everybody should have enough time to play catch once in awhile."

They went their separate ways after that, but Alec remained on Julia's mind for the rest of the evening.

She considered herself a good judge of character. As such, she'd thought she'd had Alec pegged after their meeting in her office, her opinion reinforced by the fact that he'd arrived late and had come across as both obstinate and arrogant.

Then, at the baseball diamond, he'd showed up in his snazzy two-seater, wearing a tailored suit and silk tie, and looking as out of place as a car salesman at a cyclist convention. Her initial opinion had seemed on target, especially after their conversation about his dating habits. She'd probed a bit more than usual— all of it work-related, she assured herself.

But then, once the game got under way, he'd surprised her.

Julia wouldn't say he'd ever managed to look comfortable sitting with her in the manufactured shade of the canopy. Or that he'd understood the point of a ball game in which no one kept score and even the parents on the opposing team clapped for all the little sluggers as they took their turn at the tee to bat. But he'd appeared so intrigued by it.

"Didn't you play baseball when you were a kid?" she'd asked him at one point.

His tone had been an odd combination of wistfulness and resignation when he'd replied, "Not really. Not like this."

Julia was the one intrigued then.

So, that night, after her kids went to bed, she stayed up not only to pour over her plans for his public reincarnation, but also to read his biography, both what his company had provided and what she could glean on her own from the internet.

By all accounts, Alec McAvoy had grown up in privilege—attending a couple of East Coast boarding schools before moving on to an Ivy League education with a stint abroad between his undergraduate degree in finance and his MBA in business. His paternal grandparents were old money and owned a summer home on Nantucket. From the photographs, it was far grander than the cozy beach house Julia and Scott had once dreamed about buying on Lake Michigan.

Alec's parents, meanwhile, were fixtures at parties thrown by Hollywood A-listers, socialites and European high rollers. At one point, rumors had swirled about Peter and Brooke McAvoy's finances running low, but it hadn't seemed to slow them down. On the internet, Julia ran across a picture of them snapped just six months earlier in which they were sunbathing on the deck of a yacht anchored off Corfu. The yacht belonged to a Greek shipping magnate. She also ran across photograph after photograph of the elder McAvoys among the glitterati. The pictures stretched back well over a decade. If they were broke, they were doing a poor imitation of it.

Alec, of course, was wealthy in his own right. As the CEO of Best For Baby, he earned seven figures, and then there was the not so small matter of the fortune he'd inherited from his grandfather after the man's death half a decade earlier. The silver spoon he'd been born with had never had a chance to tarnish, much less be removed.

She stared at his photo on her computer screen. Alec McAvoy had it all: wealth, good looks, lofty connections and power. He also had a PR problem the size of the *Titanic*. And that was why the Best For Baby board had hired her, Julia reminded herself as she switched off the computer just after midnight and stumbled off to bed, taking with her a printout of the damning article that had started the current controversy. She practically knew it by heart, but she wanted to be sure she hadn't missed any subtext that could be used in the rebuttal articles she planned to plant in various media outlets starting Monday.

She nodded off one paragraph in and then dreamed about him...in a not-so-professional way.

They were in her office, the door closed, the blinds at the window behind her desk pulled—not to cut the glare of the sun, but for privacy. Her hair was loose, her lips slick with red gloss. She wore a strapless, snug-fitting dress and dangerously high heels—neither of which was inappropriate for the workplace. It wasn't only the clothing that Julia didn't recognize. Who was this hypersexualized version of herself?

As for Alec, he was smiling—that smug, amused expression that managed to be both annoying and sexy at the same time.

"Come here," he said, his voice barely a whisper.

Even though Julia wasn't one to take orders, she stepped closer at his command, stopping an arm's length away. His tie was askew, his shirtsleeves rolled halfway up his arms. Her gaze wandered to his belt buckle and the revealing fit of his trousers. She wasn't quite successful at biting back a moan.

When she glanced up, his green eyes had turned molten with interest. It had been a long time since a man had looked at her that way. A long time since she'd *wanted* a man to look at her that way.

"Closer. Come closer, Julia."

This time his words were more dare than order. A shiver of excitement ran through her, followed by anticipation, as she closed the distance.

He lifted his hand, reaching for her.

"Julia," he said softly.

She jolted awake at his touch, scattering the papers that had been in her slack grip. After scrubbing a hand over her face, she gathered the printouts together and put them on her bedside table. Then she got up for a drink of water. Her throat was dry and her body was on fire. She felt foolish, juvenile. Most damning of all, she was turned on.

It was a reasonable reaction, she assured herself. An understandable response. She might be a professional consultant under contract to polish Alec's tarnished public image, but she also was a woman—a healthy, adult woman—with needs that had gone unfulfilled for a very, *very* long time. Alec was handsome and on her mind thanks to work. So, she'd dreamed about him. Big deal. It wasn't as if anything had happened while she was awake and, as such, fully responsible for her actions.

Even so, she turned on the faucet again. Instead of refilling her glass, this time she cupped her hands under the cold water and splashed it on her face.

On the way back from the bathroom, she checked on her children, stopping first in one doorway and then the one next to it. The bedrooms were identical in size and layout, with the twin beds located directly across from the door. Danielle was curled up on her side, one slim arm wrapped around her pillow. Next door, Colin was stretched out on his bed with his arms flung wide, as if he were attempting to embrace not only the room, but also the world beyond. Like his sister, he looked so relaxed, so...angelic.

Julia smiled, relieved to find her footing again. First and foremost, she was a mother. Her kids were her life. They were all she needed, she assured herself. But after she slipped back into bed, it was hard to ignore how empty the other side of it suddenly seemed.

"Alec, please. They're this season's Kellen Montgomery sunglasses," his mother whined on the other end of the line. "You're not being fair. I can't be expected to go on my trip without sunglasses."

Brooke probably had six dozen pairs of designer shades, each one pricier than the last. He didn't bother to point this out. He knew from past experience that using reason with his spendaholic mother would be futile.

It was not quite ten o'clock on Saturday morning, he was in his office, and already his left temple was starting to throb with what promised to be one doozy of a headache. Not even twenty-four hours had passed since Brooke's last call seeking funds. He'd given in then. This time, he held firm.

"No."

"You're being unreasonable," she accused.

He nearly laughed at that. Instead, he said, "No, what I'm being is *responsible*."

Brooke continued as if he hadn't spoken. "It's *our* money."

"Which Granddad has left me in charge of managing," he pointed out for the umpteenth time.

"And you're turning out to be even more of a tight-fisted killjoy than that old man was!"

Alec rubbed his temple. He could feel the blood pounding under the pads of his fingers. "Fine. I'm a tightfisted killjoy." He'd been called worse, especially lately. "Now, if there's nothing else, I need to get back to work, since apparently earning a living and then living within one's means are concepts that skipped a generation."

That barb generated a grunt of disapproval. Still, his mother's tone switched from irate to what passed for maternal concern when she said, "Seriously, Alec, I worry about you. Here it is, a Saturday morning—the *weekend*—and you're talking about work." There was a slight pause. He pictured Brooke shaking her head. "I don't know where your father and I went wrong. It's not natural, working on the weekend. Weekends are for fun. What happened between you and Laurel? She was such a nice young woman. And she knew how to have a good time. I liked her."

No wonder, he thought. Birds of a feather. His mother and Laurel had met on only one occasion and had hit it off immediately, comparing notes on their favorite designers.

"She wasn't my type." As soon as he said it, Julia

sprang to mind, which was odd. She wasn't his type, either.

"That's because Laurel had a social life," Brooke remarked sulkily.

"I guess that was the reason," he agreed, hoping to shorten the conversation.

It came as an unwelcome realization that there was some truth to his mother's barb. Laurel did know how to have fun and, just like his mother, her social life came at the expense of her children.

"They'll just be bored and in the way," Laurel had said the one time he'd asked if she wanted to bring them out to dinner.

It had been her choice to exclude them whenever they went out for an evening or away for a weekend. He'd told Julia as much. So, why did it bother him now that he'd been only too happy with her decision? Or that he couldn't help thinking that Julia Stillwell would never view her kids as being "in the way"?

Julia had strict rules against going to the office on weekends, but that didn't prevent her from doing a little work at home, as long as it didn't interfere with her children. She'd meant it when she'd told Alec that her career didn't define her, but she took her job seriously—she couldn't afford not to. It was how she'd earned her reputation, and why a company as large as Best For Baby had sought out her expertise. Sometimes that meant bending herself into the shape of a pretzel or forgoing a good night's sleep to get everything done that needed to get done. She'd long ago accepted that and made fast friends with caffeine.

So midmorning, while her kids were seated at the kitchen table, busy working on homework, she sipped freshly brewed Colombian Supreme from a mug and dialed Alec's office. She planned to leave a message on his voice mail. She had his cell number, but hadn't wanted to bother him off hours. She should have known better. He answered on the third ring, sounding distracted and slightly disgruntled at the interruption.

"McAvoy here."

Caught off guard—and with a mouthful of coffee—she sputtered after swallowing, "A-Alec. Hi. It's Julia Stillwell." She blushed, recalling the dream, and was thankful that he couldn't see her and question her on her reaction.

"Julia." There was a brief pause during which she pictured him leaning back in his chair. Was he smiling? Then he said, "I was just thinking about you."

The heat suffusing her face spread to other parts of her body at that. She didn't care for the tug of excitement his words elicited. Still, she asked, "You were?"

"Yeah. I ordered a bagel and coffee from the deli up the block more than an hour ago and the deliveryman just showed up ten minutes ago, despite the promise I'd have my order in less than thirty minutes. Clearly, he could benefit from a lecture on the importance of punctuality."

She gritted her teeth at the amusement in Alec's tone since it came her expense. But his response was just what she needed to banish that dream. "I hope you didn't tip him well."

"Actually, I did. He said his bike had a flat tire and he was apologetic."

"Well, if he was apologetic..." She left it at that, figuring she'd made her point.

"Sorry goes a long way, doesn't it?" Alec replied amiably.

"Only when it's offered immediately and is sincere."

Deep laughter rumbled. "And if I told you I had a flat tire on the way to our first meeting and that was why I was late, would you still hold it against me?"

"Did you?"

"No."

In spite of herself, she chuckled at his candid response. "You were late because you didn't want to be there, Alec. And the apology you offered was off-handed at best."

"I didn't want to be there," he agreed. "But that's not why I was late."

"Then what's your excuse?"

Several beats of silence followed. "I had to take a call from my mother."

Julia snorted. "Right."

"So cynical." He made a tsking noise. "So, what are you doing working on a Saturday? I recall someone telling me something about how work wasn't her main priority. 'It's what I do, not who I am,' or some such rebuke. But maybe I misunderstood."

She ignored the barb. "I came across a few articles that I thought you might find enlightening."

They were about child-rearing and what new parents could expect. She figured Alec could use the insight, both into what made children act the way they did and what parents went through as a result. Of course, no one really understood parenthood until they were in the trenches, living it day to day. At that point, all of the diatribes from a childless person were relegated to the trash heap.

"Are you at your office?" he asked as if she hadn't spoken.

"On a Saturday? No way." Then she couldn't resist needling him. "I may decide to slip in a little work here and there on a weekend, but, unlike you, I do it from home. While I've been surfing the internet for information, my kids have been occupied finishing up their homework."

"Homework! On a Saturday? That's worse than making a high-paid corporate executive stay late for a meeting," he told her, alluding to the remark she'd made about Alec scheduling after-hours meetings with his staff. "And you called me unpopular."

Through the beveled glass door of the closet-sized room that served as her home office, Julia could see into the kitchen. At the table, Colin was copying down his spelling words and Danielle was working on math problems. Their sour expressions made it clear that neither one of them was happy with her at the moment.

"I'll give you that, but it's now or never. We have a busy weekend in store."

"Right. Danielle has a soccer game today." Julia was surprised that he remembered. She was even more surprised when he asked, "What position does she play?"

"Goalie." Then she said, "Hey, this is good, Alec."

"What's good?"

"The polite interest you're showing in my kids. This

is exactly how you need to come off when you're out at the events I have planned."

"I'll keep that in mind." But he didn't sound happy about the suggestion. "For the record, I asked because I was interested. I'm not a completely lost cause."

She felt embarrassed, small. "I didn't mean—"

"You're just doing your job," he interrupted.

"I, um, yes. Still, if I hurt your feelings..."

"You didn't." But she wasn't so sure. Still, he was changing the subject. "So, Danielle plays goalie?"

"Yes." Since it gave her something else to talk about, Julia added, "The game doesn't start until later this afternoon, but it's going to be such a nice day that we're heading out early to meet up with some other families for a pregame picnic."

"A picnic, hmm? Grilled hot dogs, hamburgers, ants and the works?"

Alec didn't sound nostalgic so much as wistful, as if such a thing were beyond his experience. Julia supposed someone who had spent much of his adolescence at a boarding school hadn't been to many picnics. Today's get-together would be potluck. All of the team's families would bring a dish, with the coach kicking in the dogs and burgers. Her contribution was a fresh fruit salad and juice boxes. From previous experience, she knew there would be enough food to feed a small army.

She softened and was on the verge of inviting him to join them—as her client, she assured herself, not as her personal guest—when he said, "I'll think of you while I'm having a late lunch in my bug-free, air-conditioned office."

Her goodwill evaporated as quickly as it had come. And he claimed not to be a lost cause. The man was hopeless. And so not her type. The previous night's dream popped back to mind again. Whether he was her type or not that hadn't stopped her from fantasizing.

Irritated with herself and the inappropriate direction her thoughts kept taking, she made her tone purposefully brisk and businesslike when she said, "Getting back to the reason for my call, I'm emailing you the links to those articles I mentioned."

She punctuated her words by hitting the send button.

"The ones you think I might find enlightening."

"Exactly."

"I'll look forward to reading them." His tone was maddeningly benign.

"No, you won't."

"But I will read them."

"See that you do."

After that crisp response, Julia bid him goodbye.

Alec listened to the dial tone hum for a full minute after she hung up. See that you do. What? Did she plan a pop quiz for later? And the woman claimed that he was all work and no play. Well, she was a royal pain in the backside. A pretty one with her classic features and slender build, but a pain nonetheless.

Why then, he wondered, was he smiling?

By midafternoon, Alec had finished up his work and logged off his computer. The rest of the day, the evening in particular, loomed ahead of him, long and lonely. He could kill some time reading the articles Julia suggested. His lip curled in distaste just thinking about it.

You don't know how to have fun.

He wanted to be able to discount the accusation since it had come from his mother. But the fact remained that it was Saturday and he'd spent the better part of the day in his office and had no plans for the evening.

He hadn't dated much since Laurel. There was no pining involved in that decision, as he'd been the one to break things off. He'd meant it when he'd told Julia that things had run their course. No, his continuing single status had more to do with the late hours he kept at the office and, well, plain old disinterest. He hadn't met anyone engaging or exciting...bar Julia.

Alec frowned. Did she even date? She'd managed to duck answering when he'd asked if she was seeing someone. He gathered up printouts of the articles she had suggested he read and tucked them into his briefcase to go over later. All the while, a question nagged. What kind of man would she prefer? The guy would have to like kids. That much was a given. And he would have to be comfortable around them. A family man. Not someone like Alec.

He wasn't her type any more than she was his, which was why he found it damned annoying that, later that evening while he was out to dinner with a young woman he'd met in the spring at a fundraiser, he found himself thinking about Julia.

FOUR

——

Julia was the first to arrive at the office on Monday, meaning she was responsible for making the coffee. After setting it to brew, she booted up her computer. She heard the maker gurgle out the last bit of java and went to pour herself a cup. Then, seated back at her desk, she picked up the telephone and got down to work. She called Dexter Roth first, touching base with him on the progress of the marketing team's current strategy. With that marked off her lengthy to-do list, she dialed the first of several contacts she'd plucked from her bulging Rolodex.

Over the course of a decade in business, Julia had learned which ears to plant a bug in when she needed to generate buzz. Since time was of the essence, she started with the local network television affiliates. Their morning shows, which ran on soft news, were always hungry for a hot topic to pull in viewers. Thanks to his verbal gaffe, Alec was definitely that. Indeed, she was banking on the fact that he was hot enough the networks might wind up picking up the story, too, and air it nationally. That would save them time and perhaps even some travel.

By ten o'clock, she had Alec booked for that Thursday on *Rise & Shine, Chicago!* On Friday, he was set to appear on a popular Windy City radio program *The Morning Commute with Leo & Lorraine*. Julia hadn't cleared either time with him in advance. She figured she'd made it plain to him already that job number one at the moment was damage control. If that meant rescheduling meetings and finishing up paperwork on off hours, so be it. That shouldn't be a problem for him since he already worked evenings and could be found in his office on weekends.

Alec didn't sound pleased when she called him at eleven with an update on the week's itinerary.

"*Rise & Shine, Chicago*? The last time I caught that show the featured guest was a dog that had been trained to use indoor plumbing."

"I bet that generated good ratings for the show. My hope is that so will you."

"Are you comparing me to a domesticated pet?"

"I wouldn't dare."

He mumbled something under his breath.

"Bad weekend?"

"No. It was fine. I went out on a date Saturday night. You?"

He said it like a challenge.

"Home with the kids. Boring by your standards, I'm sure. We made popcorn and watched a movie."

"What was the movie?"

It almost pained her to say it…. "*Parent Trap*."

She thought she heard him chuckle. Then he was

all business. "I thought I was going to be doing events out in public."

"You will do those, too," she promised. "But the TV appearance and the radio segment will help drum up interest in the meantime and, hopefully, start to shift the current tenor of public opinion."

Again, he muttered something she couldn't quite catch, but he agreed, so she went on.

"You also may be getting a call from a *Sun-Times* reporter in the next day or two. I gave her both your office number and your cell. Her daughter attends school with mine. I ran into her over the weekend at Danielle's soccer game."

"Calling in favors?" he asked.

"I suppose it could be viewed that way, but I don't tell Lori Mercer what to write. I offer ideas that she may or may not find intriguing enough to follow up on. If she calls you, you can set up an appointment, but get in touch with me before you do the actual interview."

"Sure." He waited a beat, then asked, "Did they win?"

"Who?"

"Danielle's soccer team."

"Oh. Yes. Two to nothing." Even though it wasn't necessary, she added, "She blocked a couple of really tough shots."

"You sound proud."

"I am. Very." Julia was smiling when she glanced up to find her assistant standing in the open doorway. Sandy was holding the coffeepot, her brows raised in question. Julia didn't think the question was whether or not Julia wanted a refill. Even so, she beckoned for

Sandy to come in and held out her half-empty cup for a warm-up. For Sandy's benefit as well as her own, she got back to business. "Oh, Alec, I wanted to ask, did you get the email I sent over this morning?"

"The one on the expenses involved in child-rearing? It's been received, read and filed." His tone made it clear what he thought about it. Odds were good the file he referred to was the circular one known as the trash can.

"I sent that one over the weekend. I'm referring to the one I sent about an hour ago."

"Let me check my email." She heard clicking, then a mild expletive. "Media talking points?"

"That's the one."

"Are you kidding me?"

She considered the question rhetorical and didn't answer it. "Don't just give the article a cursory glance before setting it aside. You need to read it, study it. I want you to *memorize* it."

She was pretty sure she heard a sigh. "So, I am to stay on script at all times," he replied.

"Exactly." Julia pictured the corners of Alec's mouth pulling down in a frown. It was a nice mouth, one that had featured prominently in her dream.

"Anything else?" he asked.

"No!" She cleared her throat. "Actually, yes. I've been in touch with a couple of bloggers, including Jan Owens. Have you heard of her?"

"Should I have?"

"She trashed you big-time after the article came out."

"A lot of people did, Julia. I didn't think to take down all of their names," was his dry response.

"Yes, well, not all of them have her reach. She's one of the reasons the story went viral. She writes a blog called Mommy's Helper. Have you heard of it?"

"No. But I'm sure the company's marketing team has."

"Yes, I've talked to Dexter Roth."

"You've talked to Dexter?"

Alec's tone told her he wasn't happy to be left out of the loop. She couldn't blame him for that, so she hastened to add, "I spoke to him only this morning. I'm sure he's planning to talk to you. Now, about Jan Owens's blog, it connects stay-at-home moms with products and services that are supposed to make their lives easier and their kids healthier, happier and smarter."

"What does she do? Wield a magic wand?"

Julia chuckled. "No, but her site averages tens of thousands of hits a week, which makes her very influential when it comes to buying patterns. Not only are you *persona non grata* right now, but you've made your company a pariah among her readership, which represents Best For Baby's core customer base."

"Dexter is proposing giveaways and special offers to entice people to buy our products," he said. "Is that something he should approach her about?"

"No. It's something *you* need to approach her about. Touch base with her today, if at all possible." Julia rattled off the blog address. "You can find her contact information on there. She's on West Coast time, so keep that in mind."

"Sending me into the lion's den?" he asked wryly.

"Afraid?"

"Petrified." Though he didn't quite sound it. She pictured him smiling, maybe lounging back in his chair... shirtless. She lurched forward in her own chair and upset her coffee mug. Brown liquid spread over his file.

"Damn!"

"Everything all right?"

"Yes. I just spilled my coffee," she told him, blotting it up with some tissues.

"I hope you didn't burn yourself."

Oh, Julia felt singed, but not from the coffee. What was it about this man that kept setting her imagination into motion?

"No. I'm fine. The same can't be said for your file, I'm afraid. It's ruined."

"That may be a good thing. Maybe we need to start over."

It was an interesting thing to say. She wasn't quite sure she understood what he meant by it. "Hoping to get out of doing a guest blog?" she asked.

"Among other things."

That made things clear as mud. Several seconds ticked by as she puzzled over it.

"Julia? Are you still there?"

"Yes. Sorry." She got back to business. "Anyway, in the email I sent Jan, I told her you would love to guest blog on Friday."

"In other words, you lied." But he laughed.

"Through my teeth, or rather, my keyboard. I'll help you draft the content before you send it for posting. Plan to spend a little time monitoring the replies to your post and answering them where possible. Again, I'll help you with the responses."

"I can think of more palatable things to do on a Friday, but at least I'll have company."

"I, um, won't be *with* you."

"Figure of speech."

She knew that.

"So. If this Jan Owens is so influential, why am I not lined up to do a guest post sooner?"

"First of all, we want a Friday. They are her biggest day traffic-wise. That's when most of the giveaways occur, so more moms are likely to click in. Secondly, by then we should have a full-blown strategy in place for dealing with the public relations fallout and we can roll out parts of it."

"Clever. You've been busy," Alec remarked.

His tone held admiration now, maybe even a little gratitude, which she appreciated, since he was the beneficiary of all her hard work.

"Very busy," she agreed.

"Did you get *any* sleep over the weekend?"

The question, by itself, was innocuous...until the dream reared up from her subconscious. Need of the most basic kind settled low in her belly. Just as she had on Friday night, Julia tried to ignore it. And, just like on Friday night, she was about as successful.

Still, she managed to say in a bored tone, "I got a few winks."

"Yet you claim not to clock overtime. I think you missed your calling. Instead of being an image consultant, maybe you should teach time management. I'd send you a few of my department heads," Alec offered.

"They don't know the meaning of prioritizing or how to multitask. You're apparently a pro."

It had as much to do with luck as skill. Despite her best-laid plans, sometimes it came down to that. A feverish child, car trouble or a computer glitch could derail everything. That wasn't the sort of information one confided to a client, however. So, to Alec, she said, "I do my best to stay focused."

"Focused," he repeated. "My mother would say we both sound boring." She thought she heard ringing and then a soft oath. "Speak of the devil."

"Excuse me?"

"My mother is calling my cell. I don't want to take this, but I have to."

"I'll be in touch."

Julia might have given him points for being a dutiful son had he not sounded so grim.

It was late when Alec got to his apartment. The place wasn't home, but it was a refuge of sorts. He'd had the day from hell, with plenty of fires to put out. In addition to his mother's call and the usual raft of meetings and personnel issues, his public relations disaster was showing no signs of abating. A highly rated television show was making noise about dropping Best For Baby as a sponsor and a group of parents had begun a picket line outside the building. Their signs urged the board to Dump McAvoy among other things, and the media had been there.

Alec had hoped to sneak out through the parking garage unnoticed. They'd swamped his car until security forced them to scatter and let him pass. He could only imagine how the story would play out on the evening news.

He tossed his keys on the console and grabbed an imported beer from the fridge in the kitchen, twisting off the cap on his way to the couch. He switched on the television and channel surfed until he came to a baseball game. The phone rang as he was tugging off his tie.

"You should have called me about the picket," an irritated female voice said.

"Hello, Julia." He took a pull of his beer.

"The local news led off with it at six, and they've been teasing it for the late broadcast along with a shot of you trying to drive your Porsche through a throng of sign-waving protesters."

He pinched his eyes closed. "For the record, I didn't run anyone over."

"Alec, this is why your board hired me."

"What would you have done?" he demanded.

"At the very least, I would have had you issue a statement before you left. As it was, you looked like a criminal trying to make a fast getaway."

He exhaled. Anger warred with exhaustion. "This is ridiculous. I'm not a criminal. I said one stupid thing, and now I'm being crucified."

"I'm sorry." There was a slight pause, then she asked, "Long day?"

"Never-ending."

"Mine, too, but for different reasons." He heard a sigh.

"Yeah?"

"Nothing work-related."

He should have been relieved on that score, since

he was her main client at the moment, but he found himself curious instead. "You could still share it with me if you want."

A couple beats of silence passed. Then she admitted, "My daughter and I had a...disagreement."

"That's the same thing as a fight, right?" He laughed, hoping to get Julia to do the same, but she sounded every bit as grim as before when she replied, "Pretty much."

He studied the beer bottle and confided, "My mother and I had one of those today, too. Something must be going around."

"Gee, you mean I can look forward to this sort of thing for the next thirty years?" This time her laughter echoed through the line.

Alec didn't join in. He sipped his beer, recalling the argument he and Brooke had had over a catering charge she wanted to put on the account Alec kept at a restaurant where he was a regular. The owner had insisted Brooke have Alec call him before he would book the event—dinner for twelve aboard one of their friends' boats on Lake Michigan.

"For your sake, I hope not," he told Julia now. Even as he said it, he heard a child's voice calling "Mom" in the background. "It sounds like you're being paged."

"Always." But there was a grin in her voice.

"We'll talk again in the morning." She paused. "You'll get through this, Alec."

His name, said in such a tender tone, touched something inside him. "You almost sound like you believe that."

"I do." She cleared her throat. "I've never failed a client. I don't intend for you to be the first."

They said goodbye and disconnected. Alec finished off his beer and headed to bed. Even though it was pointless, he found himself wishing that Julia's reasons for wanting to save his hide weren't totally professional.

Julia dialed Alec's number just after ten the following morning. She'd tossed and turned half the night trying to figure out how to mitigate the damage from the protest. That wasn't the only reason she'd tossed and turned, but it was the only one she could think about without becoming flushed.

"Good morning," she said when he came on the line.

"Is it? I've already had an email from Herman Geller."

"I know. He cc'd me."

"Then you are aware that my approval rating among members of the board is bad and heading toward worse. Some of them didn't want to give me a second chance as it was. If they convince enough of their colleagues to feel the same way..." He left it at that.

"I know." Both of their jobs were on the line. "I have a plan. Clear your schedule for a few hours starting around one o'clock."

"Why?"

His voice held trepidation. She had the feeling it would hold an emotion far more unpleasant when he heard what she was about to say.

"A local mother's group is holding its annual picnic in Grant Park. I thought we could stop in for an hour or so. You could ooh and ahh over the little ones and maybe help judge the cutest baby contest at three."

After she said it, Julia held her breath. The silence was telling, but she gave Alec points for not swearing.

"Are you still there?" she asked after a moment.

"I'm here."

"Well?"

A mild oath slipped out half under his breath this time. "Is this is absolutely necessary?"

"Honestly? I don't see another way to convince the public that you're not some kind of monster without, well, making sure you are seen out and about with children."

"I get that, but can't I just make an appearance and call it good without judging babies?"

"It won't be so bad."

"I don't know the first thing about babies. They make me nervous. As it is, I'm not that good around older children."

"Oh, I don't know. You did fine with mine at the ball diamond last Friday."

Sure, Alec had been a little awkward, especially at first. Danielle didn't like him, but that wasn't because of anything he'd done. Her kids hadn't found him frightening or creepy. If they had, they would have said so. They were unflaggingly honest in that way. All kids were.

"Yeah?"

"Yeah."

"What if I wind up pelted with pacifiers or booed out of the park?"

His attempt at humor came as a welcome surprise.

Julia chuckled at the visual. "I don't think it will come to that. I know one of the organizers."

"Calling in another favor?"

"Let's just say I promised her that Best For Baby would offer a savings bond to the contest winner, and it doesn't hurt that we'll be passing out coupons for a free package of diapers."

"My reputation is being salvaged by something worn on a baby's butt. Great," he muttered. "So, you'll be there, too?"

Foolishly, her heart kicked out an extra beat. Her tone purposefully glib, she asked, "Afraid to go into the lion's den alone?"

"Hell yes. Besides, if I have to suffer through an afternoon of glad-handing and gratuitous fawning, I think you should, too."

"I don't think it will be as painful as all that," she told him. "But I promise to stick by you the entire time."

"Something to look forward to." His reply had her smiling. "Where do you want to meet?"

"How about the lobby of your apartment building in, say, half an hour?"

"My apartment building?"

"You'll need to change your clothes for this."

"And you need to approve my attire."

She neither confirmed nor denied his response. "Half an hour," she said again. "'Bye."

When Alec arrived, Julia was already in the lobby, leaning against the front desk and chatting with the security guard. It didn't surprise him that she'd beat him there, even though his office was closer. He'd been waylaid by a couple of phone calls, including one from her reporter friend. What did surprise him was her easy manner with Hank Maloney, the grizzled-looking, retired cop who stood sentinel in the apartment building's lobby Monday through Friday. Alec had lived in the building for nearly four years and he'd never heard Hank's voice, except for an occasional grunt that served as a greeting.

The older man's leathery face was split with a grin now. He had his wallet out and was showing Julia pictures of his grandkids.

"They're just precious, Hank."

"Smart as whips, too," he replied. "I've been puttin' aside some of the pension money I get from the city so that they'll be able to get into a good college someday without having to take out loans. My boy, he teaches at a parochial school. His wife, too. They started a college fund right after the kids were born, but the way tuition is rising, it ain't going to be enough."

"Tell me about it," she said grimly. She spotted Alec then and straightened. Her expression turned businesslike. "Hello, Alec."

She was dressed in navy capri pants and a floral print top that was belted at the waist with a length of satin ribbon. The blouse's butterfly sleeves fluttered as she waved goodbye to the guard and crossed the lobby to Alec. The outfit, which she'd paired with low sandals, was perfect for an afternoon of strolling about the park. He'd bet she'd changed. He couldn't see her wearing that to her office.

Girl next door, he thought. She had that appeal.

Especially when she offered a guileless smile as she stepped with him into the old-fashioned elevator. He pulled the gate closed, punched his floor and was grateful that the short elevator ride made conversation unnecessary. The way he was feeling, he was bound to say something foolish.

His apartment occupied the top floor of a turn-of-the century building that had been updated to include all of the modern amenities, such as a jetted tub, walk-in closets and a gourmet kitchen. Whoever had renovated the place had been smart enough to retain its period charm, keeping intact coffered ceilings, coved moldings and the parquet wood floors that ran throughout.

The apartment had three bedrooms and two full baths. In addition to garage parking—a luxury in Chicago, especially at lower price points—his unit came with exclusive access to a rooftop deck that afforded spectacular views of Lake Michigan. When he was home in the evenings and when Chicago's weather cooperated—neither of which happened often enough—he sat up there with a drink, lulled by the fading light that reflected off the big lake's waves. Maybe tonight, he thought. It had been a long time since he'd allowed himself to truly unwind.

After unlocking the door, he stepped back to let Julia inside. Given the lemony aroma of furniture polish, he concluded that his cleaning lady had already paid her weekly visit. He dropped his keys on the dust-free console table in the entryway and turned to face Julia. She was frowning.

"What?" he asked, noting the line that had formed between her eyebrows.

"This isn't what I expected."

"It's a little Spartan," he agreed.

Alec had never gotten around to hiring a decorator to fill it up with the kind of bric-a-brac and whatnots that made a place appear lived-in.

"Have you lived here long?"

"A few years," he admitted. When he'd signed the initial lease, Alec hadn't planned to stay in the apartment longer than a year. But time had marched well beyond that deadline. "My accountant keeps after me to purchase a house or condominium."

"Good advice."

"It makes sense from an investment point of view," he agreed.

"But?"

He shrugged. "I've looked. A lot. It's gotten so that I feel guilty for taking up so much of my real estate agent's time."

"What is it that you're after?"

It was a straightforward question, similar to the ones his agent had posed repeatedly. Was Alec after more natural light? Better storage? A high-rise view of the city? Closer proximity to his office? A house with a yard and mature trees in one of the higher-end, established neighborhoods that dotted the lakeshore?

His answers had been vague, in part because the truth was harder to share. He wanted a house or even a condo that seemed like a home. Unfortunately, he wasn't sure what a home was supposed to feel like. He'd never really had one, shuttled as he'd been during his boyhood between boarding schools and vacation spots on those rare occasions when he was invited to join his parents. His grandparents' beach house on Nantucket was as close as he'd come to ever feeling as if he belonged somewhere. Alec still owned the place, though he didn't get there often now that he lived in Chicago. So, he'd stayed in the apartment, throwing money out the window in the form of rent, or so his accountant complained.

"What am I looking for?" he repeated Julia's question now. "I'm not sure, I just know that I haven't found it yet."

"I'd like a house someday," she said then. "Something north of the city so the kids could play outside without having to make a special trip to a park."

"And with a white picket fence around a yard big enough for a golden retriever to run?"

Alec meant the question to be teasing, but the joke seemed to be on him. The Norman Rockwell-esque picture his words painted was damned appealing... and every bit as foreign as the sporty import he drove.

"Maybe." Her smile was lopsided. "Not sure about the dog, even though Colin and Danielle have been begging for one since last Christmas."

"Kids like dogs."

Her brows shot up. "Oh?"

Alec shrugged. "That's what I hear anyway."

"Did you have a dog when you were a growing up?"

"No. They weren't allowed." If he let them, the bitter memories circling around him would swoop in and swallow him up whole.

She nodded slowly. "Boarding school. Right."

He didn't care for the sympathy he saw in her expression. "Actually, I wanted an iguana for a pet when I was about Colin's age."

Her grimace made him smile. She said, "Do me a favor, and don't mention that if you see him again."

"I'll keep it to myself."

"You could have an iguana now."

Alec shrugged. "The appeal wore off a long time ago."

It sounded like she said, "Thank God."

"Besides," he added, "pets can be a lot of trouble."

"Yes. Almost as much as kids," she said wryly.

Alec clapped his hands together and decided it was time to get down to business. "So, what does one wear to judge a baby beauty contest?"

"Can I see your closet?"

Her tone was brisk and businesslike, but the way her gaze slid away made him wonder if she found the prospect of entering his bedroom as intimate, not to mention arousing, as he did.

He decided she did when Julia said in a strained voice, "You know what? Why don't you just go change into something you think is appropriate and we'll take it from there?"

"Are you sure?" He was tempting them both.

She licked her lips and he had to bite back a groan. "I'm sure."

Julia forced him to change his clothes not once but twice before she was satisfied that he'd struck the perfect balance between trustworthy corporate executive and approachable future father material.

When he returned from the bedroom the second

time, she was standing at the living room window, admiring the view of the lake. The afternoon sun teased highlights out of her butterscotch hair. For one insane moment he was tempted to brush it aside and drop a kiss on the back of her neck.

He forced his gaze to the lake and remarked, "The water looks as smooth as glass."

She turned. "According to the forecast, the evening hours will bring a storm."

"And here I'd been thinking about spending an hour or two on the rooftop deck tonight."

"That sounds relaxing. Do you manage it often?" She sounded skeptical and no wonder.

He shook his head. "Something usually comes up."

"I know the feeling. I don't often manage much alone time."

Alec wasn't thinking about being alone now. His gaze drifted briefly to her neck again, before he cleared his throat. "So, will this do?"

He spread his hands wide. He should have felt foolish. No one had dictated his attire since he'd graduated from prep school. Not that he'd strayed very much from the conservative wardrobe he'd worn back then. Instead, he felt...aware, hyperaware of the attractive woman who now studied him with a critical eye. It was a new experience for him all the way around. Most of the women Alec knew were more interested in undressing him than seeing that he was properly clothed.

"Better," she murmured, one finger tapping her lips. "The khakis are the right touch. The jeans were too informal," she said of the previous outfit. "Gabardine would be too much."

He tugged his gaze from her lush lower lip and asked, "What do you think of the shirt?"

It was maroon chambray. She'd already vetoed a short-sleeved brown polo.

She made a humming noise. "Unbutton the cuffs and turn up the sleeves."

He did as instructed and then raised his eyebrows in question. All the while that awareness sizzled.

"Hmm." Even as the sound vibrated in her throat, she was closing what remained of the gap between them. Now she stood close enough that Alec could smell the subtle scent of her perfume. It wasn't flowery or sweet. It held the tang of citrus. It enveloped him, washed over him like a wave.

"Well?"

He could barely hear the word over the blood that had begun to pound in his ears. What was wrong with him? Since when did he find intensity so sexy, or a simple touch so unsettling when she reached out and rolled up his shirtsleeves a second time?

She nodded afterward. "Yes. To the middle of the forearm makes you look more relaxed and approachable."

"Approachable," Alec repeated. He wanted to be amused. Instead, he was intrigued...and unbearably turned on.

Her hands were still on his arm, warm palms resting lightly against his bare skin. Another sizzle of awareness streaked through him, carrying the zing of an electrical current. Julia must have felt it, too, because she yanked her hands away and glanced up, her mouth rounded in surprise.

Seduction was an art, one at which Alec excelled, but he didn't plan to kiss Julia. It just happened. No other parts of their bodies connected, only their lips. That tentative brush was all the more erotic for its brevity and sweetness.

He stopped, ordered himself to take a step back, but as his mouth hovered over hers, interest turned into need, until it seemed he had no other choice but to kiss her a second time. Nothing about this meeting was brief or could be classified as sweet. Hungry would be an apt description. Desperate would fit, too. Still, he didn't touch her. He kept his arms at his sides, his hands clenched into fists. It was the only control he could muster, and even it was flagging by the time Julia broke away.

She brought her hand to her lips, her expression a mixture of surprise and, to his disappointment, horror.

"That probably wasn't a good idea," Alec said once his heart rate had leveled off.

Julia fussed with her shirt's ribbon belt. Alec wanted to fuss with it as well…unknot it so he could slip the blouse over her head. He was sucking in a breath even as she exhaled.

"No. Not a good idea. Let's not let that happen again."

Her reply made it clear she wasn't foisting all of the responsibility for that kiss on him, even if he had been the one to initiate it. She was taking responsibility, too. He wanted to agree with her about no repeats. Doing so would put both of their minds at ease. Instead, he asked, "Why not? I mean, I know it's not a good idea, but you've got to admit, that was one hell of a kiss."

In fact, he wasn't entirely certain he'd ever experienced its like. The blush that stained her cheeks made her agreement plain. When she spoke, her prim tone, even more so than her words, told him she didn't plan to come back for seconds.

"I have a job to do, Alec. I've been hired to resurrect your public image. Your board of directors is not paying me to...fool around with you in private."

He grunted out an oath. He couldn't put his finger on the source of his irritation. But like a dog with a bone, he chewed on it. "Is that your idea of fooling around? If so, you need to get out more. It entails a whole lot more than kissing."

The lips that just a moment earlier had been so soft and pliant beneath his, flattened into a thin line.

"I don't need to get out more. What I need to do is my job. Speaking of which, we need to leave now or we'll be late. I promised the organizer of the cutest baby contest that we would be at the park no later than two."

"Julia—"

She shook her head and turned on her heel. She was out of his apartment and nearly to the elevator before he had a chance to grab his keys and sunglasses and lock up. The ride down was quiet. She stood on the opposite side of the small elevator, arms crossed over her chest. No eye contact was made. It grated that she had a friendly smile and wave for Hank as she hustled across the lobby.

"You know where we're going, right?" she said once

they were outside. While his car was in the private lot designated for tenants, hers was parallel-parked up the block.

"I know where Grant Park is, and I'd imagine it won't be that hard to find the event. All I have to do is listen for the sound of crying babies," he drawled, more to irritate her than anything else.

"That's right. Crying babies." Her lips pursed and she snagged the mirrored sunglasses from his hand before he could slip them on. "You'll need to leave these off when you get there. Approachable, remember? No one wants to be looking at their reflection when they're talking to you. Eye contact is important. It tells people that you care about them. It says you're interested in what they have to say and have nothing to hide."

"Windows to the soul?" he taunted.

"For those who have one."

Alec wasn't sure whether to curse or laugh when, after giving him that lecture, she slipped on her own sunglasses.

FIVE

—

The man was infuriating. He was smug. Brash. Arrogant. Insufferable. And he was *way* too skilled with his mouth. The kiss he'd given her as they'd stood in his living room had all but caused her toes to curl.

For that reason, Julia kept the sunglasses snug on the bridge of her nose for the better part of the afternoon. Even when the sky began to darken with the first fat clouds of the evening's approaching storm, she remained hidden behind the tinted lenses. *Hidden* was a good word for it. She felt too exposed to face Alec otherwise.

Forget that foolish dream she'd had. It now paled in comparison to the real thing. What had she been thinking, letting him kiss her and then kissing him back like that? She should have pulled away at first contact. She should have *stepped* away before contact was made. His expression had made his intention plain, even if it all had happened so quickly. She couldn't plead ignorance, only insanity.

Now, no matter how hard she tried, that kiss refused to be exiled to the outer reaches of her mind. It remained front and center as the pair of them worked their way through a park packed with babies, toddlers and the harried young mothers who were running herd over them. With just a brush of his lips, he'd stoked to life the flames of a fire Julia had thought long burned out. She would be lying if she claimed not to have found Alec physically attractive from the very start, but she hadn't seen all of that heat coming. Or the need it would ignite inside her.

His words taunted her now. *Is that your idea of fooling around? If so, you need to get out more. It entails a whole lot more than kissing.*

Indeed it did.

Her friends would agree with Alec that she needed to get out more, as would her sister Eloise, who had tried more than once to fix up Julia. But Julia had too many responsibilities to take time out for romance. Besides, she was content with her life just as it was. She ignored the rebellious voice inside her head that insisted she was a liar.

"What next?" Alec asked.

"I don't know."

He frowned and she realized he was talking about what he was supposed to be doing now that the contest was over and the cutest baby had been crowned. The judging had gone surprisingly well, even if the initial reception Alec received had been on the cool side. No one had booed outright when the coordinator introduced him, but the crowd's applause had been more perfunctory than enthusiastic.

Julia cleared her throat. "What I mean to say is you should mingle and start handing out coupons."

She reached into her oversized handbag and produced a thick envelope, which she gave to him.

"Marketing emailed these over and I printed them out this morning."

He took the envelope, which he stuffed into his back pocket. "Mingle. Right."

Despite his casual attire, Alec stood out amid the crowd, in large part because he was one of the few men in attendance. All around them, mothers were scurrying after little ones who were eager to see how far and how fast their chubby legs could carry them. Children squealed in delight and cried out in frustration at being told "no."

"It's a zoo around here," Alec murmured.

Before Julia had children of her own, she might have agreed with him. "It takes some getting used to," she allowed. "For the record, though, that's exactly the sort of comment you should *not* make in public."

"I don't think I have to be worried about being overheard. I can barely hear myself think." But he lowered his voice all the same.

They made a loop of the park, circling past where a clown was transforming balloons into animal shapes. A little farther down, children were lined up to have their faces painted. When they reached the hot dog stand, Alec asked, "Want something to eat?"

"It's tempting since I didn't have lunch, but I think I'll pass."

"You haven't eaten?" He frowned. "It's after two o'clock."

The reminder was unnecessary. Julia's empty stomach knew exactly what time it was. In fact, it had been protesting at nearly audible levels for the past couple of hours. "I'll grab something before I pick up my kids from school."

"Does Colin have a T-ball game tonight?"

"No, but Danielle has soccer at five-thirty."

He glanced up. While the sky directly overhead remained blue, purple-hued clouds were crowding in from the west. "I don't think the rain is going to hold off that long."

"I have a feeling you're right."

"A free night, then," he replied.

She shook her head and tried not to focus on his mouth. "Probably not. The teams play rain or shine. Throw in some thunder and lightning, though, and it's a different story. The refs will cancel a match in short order if there's an electrical storm."

"Are you rooting for a bolt or two then?"

One side of Alec's mouth lifted after he said it, drawing her attention to his lips once again. Lightning bolts. She'd experienced a few of those earlier. Enough to remind her exactly what she'd been missing. Julia swallowed.

"You know, now that I think about it, I wouldn't mind something to drink." Suddenly, her throat was parched.

"Come on then. I'll buy."

The man who stood behind the stainless steel pushcart selling refreshments had a shaved head, pierced eyebrows and a scraggly goatee that reached nearly to his Adam's apple. Asian symbols of some sort were tattooed on either side of his neck, and both of his arms were heavily inked from wrist to shoulder and likely beneath the sleeveless T-shirt he wore. He would have been right at home working a traveling carnival, but his smile was warm and his demeanor not at all intimidating when they stepped up to order. It just went to show that appearances could be deceiving, Julia thought, even if image was everything in her business.

Her gaze slid to Alec and the outfit he was wearing. She'd picked it out, each piece chosen for the image it would project and the emotional response it would garner. What he was wearing said: *I'm safe. You can trust me.* Again, she thought, appearances could be deceiving. Alec wasn't safe. She couldn't trust him. Or more aptly, she couldn't trust herself when she was around him.

"Do you know what you want?" Alec asked. His hand came to rest on the small of her back as he spoke.

She frowned. "I can't seem to decide." Which was so not like her.

"Maybe it would help to look at the menu board," he suggested.

Julia gave her forehead a mental slap. "Right. Um, a diet cola and a plain soft pretzel will do."

Alec ordered a regular soda for himself as well as a bratwurst heaped with sautéed peppers and onions. She tried to eat healthy, but her mouth watered when he handed her the brat to hold while he fished out his wallet. He paid for their purchases and smiled knowingly as he took back the brat.

"Are you sure you don't want a little bite?"

She shook her head and brushed some of the salt off her pretzel.

"Come on," he coaxed. His tone was low and seductive. "You know you want some."

Did she ever, though to her mortification, she wasn't thinking about food. For the second time that day, her willpower pulled a disappearing act and she gave in to temptation.

"Maybe just one bite," she murmured.

His smile was smug until she bit into the brat. Then his expression faltered. Was that kiss on his mind, too?

"You've got a little..." He motioned with his index finger before reaching over with a napkin and dabbing at the corner of her mouth.

She couldn't be sure the heat burning in her cheeks was solely the result of embarrassment. Regardless, it didn't slip his notice.

"You're blushing."

"I'm not blushing. It's...it's hot out here," she replied and fanned her face for effect. It wasn't exactly a lie, even if it wasn't the whole truth.

"I'll say," Alec mumbled.

He took a sip of his soda and then tossed it and the rest of his brat in a nearby garbage can. His gaze was on her mouth again. His head was dipping down. *Uh-oh*. She knew that look. She knew what it meant and exactly what would happen next, even though she thought she'd made the boundaries of their relationship clear mere hours earlier. It didn't escape her notice that she wasn't backing away. Indeed, her chin lifted. If he kissed her again, she knew she was going to kiss him right back.

Help!

It arrived in the form of a wayward preschooler holding a dripping chocolate ice cream cone. The little boy barreled into Alec's leg. The contact caused the scoop of ice cream to fall off the cone and left a sticky brown smudge on Alec's pants just above his knee. The pants may have been khaki and casual, but their fit screamed designer. The child's mom was there in an instant, pulling out a moistened wipe.

"Sorry about—" Her apology ended on a sharp intake of breath as she recognized Alec. "Oh, my gosh! You're...you're..."

She grabbed her child and started to back away. Under other circumstances, the woman's reaction might have been comical. But since this was exactly the sort of knee-jerk response Julia had been hired to preempt, her heart sank.

"It's all right," Alec replied, but he didn't look happy. Whether about the accident or the interruption, she couldn't be sure.

Wide-eyed, the woman said, "I really am sorry. He wasn't watching where he was going."

"No harm done." Alec's accompanying laughter came out strained, seeming to negate his words.

It was little wonder the woman didn't appear convinced. "But your pants—"

"Can be washed," he finished.

He crouched down until he was nearly eye level with the boy and studied the empty cone. "It's a shame about your son's ice cream, though."

At Alec's mention of the cone's sorry state, the little boy sent up a wail so shrill and loud that it rivaled an emergency vehicle's siren. All of the moms in the immediate vicinity, turned, first to ensure that it wasn't their child in distress, and then to see what all the fuss was about. Their eyes honed in on the boy before shifting to the man next to him. The man who now held an empty ice cream cone.

Alec shot to his feet. In addition to looking guilty, his expression revealed mounting panic as the murmurs around them began to crescendo. Julia felt panicked, too. All of the afternoon's goodwill would be undone if she didn't do something and quick.

"Offer to buy him another cone," she insisted through a manufactured smile. She wasn't sure Alec heard her. The little boy was still crying, although not quite as loud.

Any hope that the worst was over was dashed when a woman standing nearby yelled out, "Hey, it's that guy who hates kids."

Alec blinked. "I don't hate—"

"What did you do to him?" a heavyset woman pushing a stroller with twins in it demanded.

"I didn't do anything," Alec replied, spreading his hands wide. His claim went over like a lead balloon when the woman spied what was in Alec's hand.

"You took his ice cream cone?" she asked incredulously. She didn't wait for a response. She hollered to the gathering crowd, "Mister Corporate Big Shot here swiped the kid's ice cream!"

Alec's humorous prediction of being pelted with pacifiers no longer seemed quite so outlandish.

"He didn't take anyone's ice cream," Julia began in a reasonable tone only to have her protestation drowned out by another woman shouting, "If he doesn't like kids, why did he come here today?"

"Because he wants us to buy his company's products," another one yelled. "I saw him judging the contest earlier. Probably it was rigged."

"Best For Baby," another mom sniffed. "More like Best for Daddy Warbucks here."

"I have some coupons," Alec began, apparently remembering the envelope Julia had given him. He pulled it from his back pocket, a drowning man reaching for a life ring.

"I wouldn't use your products if you gave them to me free," the heavyset woman who'd started everything hollered. Which took the wind out of Alec's sails since the coupons were for free diapers.

"Yeah!" another mom said.

Others were nodding in agreement.

Out of the corner of her eye, Julia caught sight of a television news crew wending its way through the agitated crowd. Great. Just great. She'd called the media before they'd set out today, giving them the tip that Alec would be in the park. Where were the reporter and her cameraman when Alec was doing a bang-up job of judging the cutest baby contest? Why couldn't they have caught *that* on tape?

As far as Julia could tell, she and Alec had two choices. They could hold their ground and run the risk that the crowd would become even more taciturn. Or they could retreat and at least ensure that an interview with a sputtering and thunderstruck Alec, holding onto a packet of diaper coupons, wasn't the highlight of the evening news.

"Let's go." She tossed out her soda and pretzel and started in the opposite direction.

"We need to clear up the misunderstanding," he said.

"We'll do that later. Right now, we need to get out of here before you end up the top story on the evening news for a second night in a row." She pointed to the news crew.

Alec muttered a mild oath. Unfortunately, the little boy heard it. He pointed a chubby finger at Alec and shouted, "Mommy, he sweared!"

"Come on," Julia cried. Looping her arm through his, she pulled him away, not stopping until they were clear of the crowd.

Once they were back where they'd parked their cars, she sucked in a deep breath and admitted, "That didn't go as I hoped."

"Talk about an understatement." Alec no longer looked shell-shocked. He was angry, as his glacial tone proved. "If this is your idea of resuscitating my image, sweetheart, I'm dead on arrival."

Julia's pride bristled at his words, even if she couldn't dispute them. He was right, and it wasn't only his image on the line now. Her credibility and reputation were in serious jeopardy if she mucked up a job this substantial.

That didn't stop her from saying, "Don't call me sweetheart."

His use of the pet name was belittling, but it rubbed against the grain for a more personal reason. Scott had called her that.

"Is that all you've got to say?" Alec demanded.

Hands on his hips, he shook his head and then rolled his eyes skyward. "I might as well hand in my resignation now. The board will be demanding it after this fiasco gets out."

"It's not going to get out." But her response lacked conviction and they both knew it. She added more damage control to her lengthy list of things to do.

Alec raked his fingers through his hair. "I'm wasting my time here. I've got real work to do—while I still have a job."

"Alec—"

He shook his head. "Forget it."

He was in his car, the two-seater's engine revving to life, before she had a chance to stop him. The man was impossible! It was just Julia's bad luck that, in this instance, he was right. She climbed into her car on a sigh. She'd blown it.

Glancing back at the park, an idea formed. What if...?

Even before Alec reached his office, he knew he owed Julia an apology, if for no other reason than leaving in the fashion that he had. He'd stomped away like an angry child. He was mad, all right, and he had good reason to be. But the situation wasn't her fault. At least not entirely.

He called her office, only to be told by her secretary that Julia was still out, so he tried her cell. It went directly to voice mail. Over the next couple of hours, he placed several more calls to her with the same results. The crow he needed to eat wasn't going to be any more palatable with the passage of time, but it was damned hard to apologize when he couldn't reach her.

He considered showing up at her daughter's soccer game that evening. He knew Julia would be there, cheering on her child, despite the day she'd had. Part of him was amazed that she could compartmentalize her life in such a fashion, keeping the various facets separate. His personal and professional lives overlapped so frequently that it was sometimes difficult to determine where one began and the other ended. Married to his job, Julia had said. The quip had annoyed him at the time, but that made it no less true.

Just before five, fat drops of rain splattered against his office window. Julia said her daughter's team would play rain or shine. Alec decided to chance it.

It was coming down harder by the time he reached the park where the soccer fields were located. Since there was no sign of lightning, the lot was full of vehicles. He wasn't sure which field her daughter was playing on, much less what her team's jerseys looked like. He was drenched to the skin by the time he stumbled across Julia's canopy. Not surprisingly, it was standing-room-only underneath it. Instead of supplying shade today, the covering offered protection from the rain, and Julia was sharing it with as many other spectators as possible.

"Julia!" he called.

She was wearing the same outfit she'd had on earlier, with the addition of a lightweight jacket. Her clothes looked damp, as did her hair, which was now pulled back into a ponytail. Her eyes widened when she saw him and she stepped around the other spectators to the edge of the canopy.

"What are you doing here?" she asked.

Neither her expression nor her voice inflection hinted at whether she was happy to see him. Feeling suddenly awkward, he joked, "It seemed like a nice night for a game."

On the field behind them Danielle's team scored. The crowd under the canopy erupted in cheers. Since there was no more room beneath the shelter, Julia pulled up her hood and stepped out into the rain.

"You're getting drenched," she remarked.

Alec shrugged. "I'll survive."

"I was going to call you after the game."

"I've been calling *you* all afternoon."

Her brow wrinkled at that. "The battery on my cell died. You have?"

He nodded. "To apologize. I acted, well, like a big jerk. I'm sorry."

"I'm sorry, too."

He accepted her apology with a nod that caused rainwater to sluice down his cheeks.

"This is ridiculous."

She ducked back under the canopy, squeezed past an older couple. A moment later, she emerged with an umbrella in hand. It was small, it's handle molded into the shape of a popular superhero. Colin's, he decided. After opening it, she lifted it over both of their heads, revealing an image of the same caped good guy that the handle sported.

"That's better," she murmured.

Alec had to agree, not only because he was now

shielded from the rain, but also because of their forced proximity. He swore he could feel the heat emanating from her body. To take his mind off that, he said, "I'm almost afraid to watch the news tonight."

"I wouldn't be." Her dimpled smile was sly. He doubted she realized it also was sexy.

"What do you mean by that?"

"Oh. Just that after you left, I went back into the park and worked a little magic."

"But you said we needed to leave."

"*You* needed to leave. The news crew and that band of riled-up mothers would have devoured you like a pack of hungry wolves. But my face isn't recognizable or all that memorable."

Alec fought the urge to disagree. Even now, partly obscured by her hood, Julia had the sort of face that was hard to forget.

"So, what kind of magic did you work?"

"I found the mother of the little boy who ran into your leg." Her expression turned wry. "Not an easy venture given how many people were milling about, let me tell you. Anyway, I talked to her, explained how unfair it was that people were jumping to conclusions and telling the reporter an inaccurate and unflattering version of events."

"And?"

"She agreed to talk to the reporter."

"On the record?"

"Better than that. On the air." Julia's smile bloomed in full. "I was there for the short interview. No matter how the clip gets edited, you should be fully exonerated. She made it clear that her child ran into you and was crying because his ice cream fell off the cone and that you had been nothing but understanding."

Alec heaved a sigh. He meant it when he said, "That's a huge relief. I wasn't looking forward to facing the board again so soon."

Had a negative news segment aired that evening, he had little doubt that, coming so quickly on the heels of the previous day's PR fiasco, another emergency meeting would have been called to reassess his future.

"Neither was I."

"I owe you."

As he said it, Alec tugged at one of the laces hanging down from her hood. He was tempted more than he wanted to be to lean down and kiss her again. The eyes regarding him were wide and watchful. He thought he saw interest flicker in them. He knew he'd seen it earlier. In the park. Before the ice-cream-cone incident.

"Three bucks."

He blinked. "Excuse me?"

"Three bucks. That's what you owe me. I bought the boy another ice cream cone. You can settle up with me later," Julia said on a smile.

"Count on it."

"Ice cream! I want ice cream!" This shout came from Colin, who tried to join them under the tiny umbrella. The boy scooted between them, dimples so like his mother's flashing with his smile.

Alec smiled too, even though he was forced to step back. Once again, he found himself out in the rain.

SIX

———

The sun was shining, the birds were singing and Julia was grinning like a kid on Christmas morning when she dialed Alec's number just after nine the following day.

"So, what did you think of the news report?" she asked as soon as he came on the line.

"I think that three bucks I owe you for ice cream will be the best three bucks I've spent in a long time. That woman's interview was pure gold."

Julia's grin widened. It was indeed.

"Don't forget the quotes from the mother whose daughter won the cutest baby contest."

"How could I? She thinks I'm misunderstood." He sounded amused.

"Yes and, according to her, all you need is the love of a good woman and a child of your own to make your reformation complete."

"That's what all women think," he said on a laugh.

Julia pictured him rolling his eyes. What she couldn't picture was Alec walking the floor with a colicky infant in the wee hours of the morning. Or sitting up with a feverish toddler or even having the patience to pitch a ball to a little boy just learning the basics of America's pastime. Which was disappointing. For him. Her smile dimmed.

"That's *not* what all women think," she replied.

"Oh? What about you?"

She swallowed. And nearly a minute of silence ticked by. At last, she managed to say, "Love is pretty powerful." Old memories beckoned. Enough time had passed so that the sharp pain that once had accompanied them was now more of a dull ache. "And children, raising them is hard work, but the rewards are, well, you have to be a parent to truly understand."

Yes, she was definitely disappointed for Alec that he wasn't interesting in discovering those rewards firsthand.

"Can I ask you something personal?"

"I suppose."

"What happened between you and your husband?"

"What happened?"

"That's too rude. I guess what I'm really wondering is, how long have you been divorced." When a couple of beats of silence followed, he said, "Never mind. You don't need to—"

"Scott died. Cancer."

At one time even saying the words would have sent her to her knees. Time didn't heal all wounds, but it made them tolerable.

A lively curse came through the line.

"God, Julia. I'm sorry. I thought...I *assumed* you were divorced."

Most people did and sometimes Julia let them. It was easier, somehow. Death was difficult to discuss, especially when it had come prematurely and after such a bitter fight for survival. It made people uncomfortable. It made *her* uncomfortable. The last thing she wanted was to be the object of someone's pity. Nor did she want her children to be.

"No. I'm widowed. Four years now."

"Sorry," Alec said again.

Everyone was, including Julia. The unfairness of Scott's death was something she would never accept, but she had moved on.

"Your kids, they were so little," Alec said.

"Scott died the week after we registered Danielle for kindergarten. Colin was a toddler."

"That must have been hard."

"It was at first," she admitted. It still wasn't easy, although she'd gotten better at single parenthood. She meant it when she told Alec, "In a way, my kids have been my salvation."

They had kept Julia moving forward, forced her to return to the business of living. Not only had her children needed her love and guidance, but they'd also needed to be fed and bathed, read to and watched over—the sort of basic care that she might have been tempted to deny herself if she weren't also a mother.

Mundane tasks such as washing dishes and going to the grocery store had provided a life raft of sorts. At first, Julia had grabbed on to it for her kids' sake much more than her own. Eventually, she'd found land again. Yes, her kids had been her salvation. They still were.

"You really mean that." Awe. That was what Julia heard in Alec's tone.

"Of course I mean that." She wanted to tell Alec that someday he would have children of his own and not only discover but also come to understand unconditional love. Unfortunately, she doubted he would agree. So, she said, "It helps that my family is nearby and so supportive."

Julia figured that would be the end of it. This was boggy territory at best.

"You're lucky. Not everyone has parents they can count on."

The statement was made with such authority and conviction that she couldn't help but be intrigued. And since he'd asked her a personal question, she didn't feel as awkward in inquiring, "Do your parents live in Chicago?"

This was met with a snort and a short pause. "They have a base of sorts in town. They keep rooms at the Westmore Hotel. They travel. A lot."

"Oh." Not sure what else to say, Julia added, "It's nice that they choose to be near you between trips."

Again the snort. "Nothing nice about it. I hold the purse strings, and I didn't give them a choice."

"I see."

"No, you don't." He sighed. "You're too...nice to see. I may not know you very well, but I can tell you're too... selfless to understand people like my parents."

It wasn't only bitterness she heard in his voice, but pain. "Alec, I didn't mean to pry. I—"

"It's all right." That glimpse of vulnerability was gone and he continued dispassionately, "You may as well know the truth. My parents have no actual income. They're too busy living the good life to bother to earn a living. They burned through every penny they had a dozen years ago. They lost their house and other property holdings. Their cars were repossessed. Even faced with bankruptcy, they refused to rein in their spending. My grandfather bailed them out. When he died, if he hadn't left his money in a trust, which he named me to administer, they'd have gone through that, too. They wouldn't be out on the streets. They're too good at leaching off of their friends for that. But..."

She pictured him shrugging, but she didn't buy his indifference.

"I don't know what to say, Alec."

Her initial assessment of him as selfish and privileged unraveled a bit more. His life hadn't been as easy as she'd assumed. She liked the man she now saw, both the compassion he'd exhibited when they spoke of her late husband and the vulnerability he was trying to hide. She told herself it would make her job all that much easier if he truly were a sympathetic figure and, as that young mother had told the television reporter, merely "misunderstood." But it also made Julia uneasy on a level she didn't want to think about, because it made falling for him that much easier, too.

"It's not something I choose to advertise, but it's not some deep, dark secret, either. It is what it is."

It also was what had shaped him and created a man who now viewed family life with such skepticism and suspicion. An ache formed in her chest. As tempting as she found it to try to convince him otherwise, this wasn't the time, nor was it her place. She decided it best to change the subject.

"I've heard from Herman Geller. No email this time. An actual call." The board's chairman had left a message at her office even before Julia arrived. He'd been effusive in his praise.

"That makes two of us," Alec said. "Thank you, again. My job is still hanging by a thread, but at least I have that thread."

"It's all in a day's work." The bored tone she used elicited the laugh she'd hoped for. "Speaking of work, we need to go over what to expect for your interview on *Rise & Shine, Chicago!* And Friday's radio program, too." Both would be airing live.

Alec sighed. "I suppose you're going to want to give me wardrobe pointers again?"

He sounded about as disgruntled as Colin did at bath time. Julia would have smiled had she not recalled what had occurred right after the last time she'd helped him pick out his wardrobe.

"Maybe," she said.

"I've got a meeting in fifteen minutes. Can we get together for lunch? My treat," he offered. "I may even throw in an ice cream cone since I owe you for one."

"Tempting." And it was in ways that she wasn't ready to consider. "But I have to be up at my children's school. It's lunch-with-loved-ones day."

"Lunch with...?" She heard him expel a breath. "All right. We could do it by phone. I'll give you a call later. Say one o'clock?"

If it were only for his Friday stint on *The Morning Commute with Leo & Lorraine*, Julia would have agreed.

But… "It really needs to be in person, Alec, since Thursday's is a televised interview. Body language carries a lot of weight. We often send signals that we don't intend."

"Is that so?" Was she imagining the challenge she heard in his voice? Regardless, she ignored it and the unsettling effect it had on her pulse.

"I can swing by on my way to lunch." He wasn't exactly on her way, but she would make it work. "Will eleven o'clock be okay for you? It shouldn't take too long. I'm thinking half an hour tops. You've been going over the talking points, right?"

"I know how to talk, Julia." His tone was suddenly taciturn.

"Alec—"

"Eleven o'clock. See you then." He hung up.

Disgruntled, she thought again. But this time, it wasn't a little boy she was imagining. It was a fully grown and way-too-handsome man, who, just the day before, had kissed her with the kind of skill and passion she hadn't experienced in a very long time.

Lunch with a loved one. Alec tapped his pen on the desk blotter. He wanted to be irritated with Julia for putting off business for something so, well, trivial. But he couldn't be. The very fact that he was playing second fiddle to her kids made him like her all the more.

His parents had rarely visited him at school. In fact, he'd spent the majority of his birthdays alone since they fell while school was in session. Sometimes his grandfather, health permitting, had come to take Alec out for dinner. But it wasn't the same as having his parents, in particular his mother, who'd given birth to him, acknowledge the occasion. He got cards from them, often a week or so late, mailed from some exotic location. And money, hefty checks written from the bank accounts his folks had been so busy depleting. He would have traded every penny for their time.

Even now, his parents' calls and visits were rare and rarely social. Brooke and Peter contacted him when they needed money. Other interaction was limited. And strained.

Lunch with a loved one. He couldn't fathom his parents interrupting their overbooked social lives to accommodate such an occasion. Julia was interrupting her jam-packed workday.

He'd meant it when he told her she was lucky to have supportive parents. Her kids were lucky, too. Even as a single mother, she was there for them, contorting herself into the shape of a pretzel if need be to ensure they understood their importance. She'd had her parents as an example. Alec didn't want to think about the example his parents had set for him. They'd failed him. He would be damned before he would fail a child the same way.

He shoved the thought away and got back to work. Between paperwork and phone calls, however, he kept glancing at his watch, eager for eleven to roll around, even if he wasn't looking forward to being schooled on what to wear, what to say and how to act during his upcoming television interview.

Body language. It was interesting that Julia had brought that up. He'd picked up a few signals from her that she probably wasn't aware she'd sent. He knew interest when he saw it. And then there was the not so small matter of their kiss. Sitting at his desk, he thought about it now, focusing not on his actions, but rather her response, in particular that little sigh that had escaped just before things ended. Oh, she'd wanted more.

Besides the obvious, what did he want? It was a question he couldn't answer. One that, frankly, he'd never asked himself where a woman was concerned. It made him uncomfortable now, edgy.

When the appointment time came and went and there was no sign of Julia, edgy became irritable. So much for her punctuality-is-rule-number-one diatribe. The niggling concern developing over what might be the cause of her tardiness only ticked him off more. What if something had happened to her? What if something had happened to her kids? He was dialing her cell number for the fifth time when his secretary buzzed.

"Mrs. Stillwell is here. Shall I show her in?"

Alec was tempted to keep her waiting, if only to reel in his emotions, but given how tight both of their schedules were, he didn't have the luxury. "Yes, Linda."

Julia was dressed in cocoa-colored trousers and a fitted cream blazer. The outfit would have been staid if not for the pop of color and animation a ruffled coral silk blouse provided. As pulled-together as her outfit was, she was anything but. Her hair was windblown, she was out of breath and a slight sheen of perspiration dotted her forehead. That concern was back in spades when she all but collapsed into one of the chairs opposite his desk.

"You're late." If she had not looked so uncharacteristically flustered, the words would have been an accusation. Instead, some of that concern leaked into his tone.

"I know. I'm so sorry, Alec. Both that I'm late and that I didn't call to let you know I was running behind schedule."

"Is every thing all right?"

"Car trouble." She laughed humorlessly and pushed the hair back from her damp forehead. "And phone trouble."

"A double whammy."

One side of her mouth lifted into a wry smile. "You don't realize how much you rely on both until you have neither. I think I need a new battery in my phone. It's not holding a charge. I realized it was dead when I tried to call you after my car overheated on the drive over."

He took in her appearance again. "How far did you have to walk?"

"Walk? No, no, no. I ran."

"You're wearing heels."

"I narrowly missed a broken ankle after one of them got caught in a sewer grate." A rueful smile accompanied the admission.

He pictured her rushing down busy sidewalks, politely pushing her way past ambling tourists and quick-paced professionals in her fashionable shoes and nearly smiled.

"Where is your car now?"

"Being towed to a garage." She shook her head. The line between her eyes spoke as eloquently as her words when she said, "It's my own fault. The temperature gauge has been blinking on and off for a week."

"You ignored it?" Julia seemed so on top of everything all the time that he found that hard to believe.

Her tone had turned slightly defensive when she replied, "When that happened last winter, I took it in to a mechanic twice. It wound up being a gauge malfunction both times, so I thought...never mind." She gathered her hair behind her neck before letting it loose again, and huffed out a sigh. "This isn't your problem, but it will affect our meeting. Even though I'm late, I need to wrap up quickly so I can make it to school."

Lucky kids, he thought again. She wouldn't disappoint them.

"How do you propose to get there? Will you run again?" While her heels weren't as impractical as some of the footwear he'd seen women don, they were a far cry from a pair of sneakers.

"I'm thinking a cab this time," she replied dryly.

By cab or foot, how Julia got to her lunch-with-a-loved-one date wasn't Alec's problem. She was right about that. But he still found himself offering, "I can take you."

Even more than wanting to help her out, he didn't want her kids to be left to wonder when or if their mother would show up. No kid should have to wonder that.

"Oh, no. Really. It's an imposition." She shook her head and a few wilted locks of hair fell into her eyes. Had Alec been closer to her, he might have been tempted to brush them away.

"I don't mind. And..." Because his thoughts kept

wanting to stray into personal territory, he added, "On the drive over we can discuss those talking points."

She made a humming sound before nodding. "Okay. That's a good idea. Thank you."

"No problem."

"I mean it," she stressed.

The hair fell back into her eyes. This time, Alec went with his impulse, and, coming around his desk, reached out to brush it aside.

"You're a good mother, Julia."

"I try."

"And that's exactly why you are. I'm happy to help." His hand had lingered at the side of her face. He pulled it back now on a sigh and surprised them both by admitting, "We'd better start talking business or I'm going to want to kiss you again."

Julia's heart beat out in triple time after he said that. She was flustered and flattered and...conflicted. Julia the image consultant didn't want Alec to kiss her again. Julia the woman very much did. Indeed, that Julia wanted Alec to do a lot more than kiss her. Like Sleeping Beauty, she'd been awakened from a long slumber. Part of her was eager to make up for lost time. The more practical part, however, knew caution was in order.

"How about we start with what you should wear," she managed to say in a voice that sounded only slightly strained.

"Good idea." Alec's expression, however, didn't match his words. And no wonder. "What the hell," he muttered and leaned forward.

This kiss was brief, a close cousin of chaste. Even so, it stirred her blood.

"Don't expect me to apologize," he warned afterward.

"I...I..."

While she stammered, a smug smile creased his cheeks.

"Back to business," he said. She was hardly reassured when he winked and added, "For now."

It took fifteen minutes to hammer down the appropriate clothing for Alec's television appearance. It helped Julia's concentration that he'd retreated to his side of the desk once again and that the intimate look he'd sported had turned pensive to the point of brooding.

"I know for other events I've said you need to come across as more accessible to your core customer base, but in this instance, I'm thinking your attire needs to reflect your position of authority."

"In other words, a suit and tie."

"You look really good in them." His brows rose and she felt her cheeks heat. "A-and they make sense since you're representing the company and the board of directors. You're reaching out to stockholders as well as consumers. Also, the host of the morning show will be wearing professional attire. If we go too casual, it might seem as if you're not taking either your position or the interview seriously."

"So, I should wear what I wear every day to the office. Something like this." He splayed his hands out in front of him, and she was forced to look at him.

He had on a cobalt-blue dress shirt and black, gray

and light blue-striped tie, knotted in a half Windsor. Draped over the back of his chair was a black suit coat. The gabardine held the faintest hint of a pinstripe. Alec had impeccable taste and wore clothes well thanks to a well-honed physique. It didn't hurt that his affluence afforded him the luxury of custom-made garments that were guaranteed to fit his athletic frame. Her mouth threatened to start watering as her thoughts turned to what the body beneath those garments might look like...and feel like under her hands. Work, she reminded herself. They were talking about work.

She cleared her throat. "Almost."

"Almost?"

"I was thinking a pastel-hued shirt underneath charcoal gabardine." But that wasn't all she was thinking, making her ever so grateful that Alec was incapable of reading minds.

"Pastel?" His lips pulled back in a sneer as he all but spat out the word, and he crossed his arms.

Julia was grateful for the fight she sensed coming. Better the two of them butt heads than dance around their mutual attraction.

"You need something softer."

"I prefer bold colors."

"Yes, well, I prefer mild winters, but that's not what I get living in Chicago."

He wasn't done arguing. "White then."

She shook her head. "Too stark and, frankly, unimaginative."

"Is that another way to say boring?"

"Oh, not at all." But, given the way his brows lowered, she suspected he didn't believe her.

"I won't wear pink, so don't even ask."

The color wouldn't suit him, but the devil made her say, "I suppose lavender is out of the question, too?"

A snort served as his reply. Oh, they were butting heads all right. It was just her bad luck that she found *that* to be a turn-on, too.

"Yellow might make your complexion appear sallow, especially on camera. Sea-foam-green is popular right now. What do you think?"

"I don't like green, in the shade of sea foam or otherwise."

"That's a very broad assertion."

"Bad association."

She waited for Alec to expound on that or at least crack a smile. He didn't. He was dead serious. What did he have against green? Something in his gaze kept her from asking.

"Light blue it is," she said. "Do you already have a shirt in that color?"

"I do. Six, as a matter of fact."

Six light blue shirts? This despite claiming he preferred bold hues. She could only imagine how many of *those* he owned. Or, for that matter, how large his closet must be to accommodate such an expansive wardrobe. Unfortunately, thinking about his closet had her thinking about his apartment. In particular, it had her thinking about his bedroom. Not merely what it looked like, but what it would be like to be in there with him, alone, with no outside responsibilities to intrude and satisfying long-forgotten needs her sole concern.

Because her rusty libido was busy undressing him, Julia made herself focus on doing the opposite.

"Now, for your tie. I'm thinking a darker shade of blue, perhaps with a small geometric print. Nothing too loud or busy."

At his comically appalled expression, she added, "Sorry. I don't know what I was thinking. Understated is your middle name."

Alec was definitely conservative when it came to his clothes and the neat cut of his hair. She glanced at his desktop with its leather blotter. Precise. Structured. Orderly. Those were traits she appreciated, even if she didn't always get to apply them in her own life. Raising kids required organization, but it also demanded flexibility. Could he be flexible?

"It doesn't matter." He frowned and no wonder. Julia rose to her feet. "We should be going."

On the drive over to the school, she planned to talk about the importance of facial expressions and hand gestures, and how both could be misinterpreted, but she got distracted as soon as she was ensconced in the leather bucket seat of his sports coupe. Nothing about the little black number could be labeled conservative. It was sleek, unapologetically sexy. It made her feel the same way. When Alec turned the key in the ignition, the engine let out a throaty growl. The sound was raw power.

"This is some car." And it was, if impractical. By their very nature, two-seaters were. Still, she was enjoying sitting in it, and couldn't help thinking that every once in awhile a little impractical indulgence wouldn't be a bad thing. And not just when it came to modes of transportation. Her gaze slid to Alec.

"Not exactly understated, hmm?" He sent Julia a wink that for all of its casualness still had her pulse picking up speed.

"Not exactly," she agreed.

"Want to drive?"

She moistened her lips. "I don't think that would be a good idea."

"Worried about your image?"

"More like I'm worried about the Porsche's gears. I haven't driven a manual transmission in over a decade," she replied.

He nodded slowly. "That's a long time."

"You have no idea," she muttered.

"Another day we'll remedy that. If you're game, that is. I'd be happy to give you a refresher course. It will all come back to you."

"Maybe." Even that equivocation seemed bold, since, based on the interest reflected in his green eyes, they weren't just talking about cars, gears and test drives.

Thanks to an accident that further snarled the already heavy midday traffic, they arrived at St. Augustine School just after the appointed time. Alec wouldn't have minded the delay—he was enjoying his time with Julia—but her kids were waiting for her. She was unbuckling her seat belt and gathering up her belongings before Alec came to a full stop at the curb in front of the entrance.

He knew better than to think she would wait for

him to come around and open the door for her, but he prevented her from jumping out by asking, "Will you need a ride back to your office afterward?"

She shook her head. Wayward curls bobbed. "That's all right. You don't need to wait. I'll catch a cab. Thanks again." After she got out, she leaned down to smile back at him through the open door. "I'll call you later. I'd feel better if we went over the talking points one more time."

Alec wanted to be more irritated than he felt. What did it say about him, he wondered, that he was actually looking forward to it?

He refused to think about it. Likewise, he refused to think about what meaning might be attached to the fact that, just up the block, when he spied a parking space, he pulled into it and placed a call to his secretary.

"I'm going to be out of the office for the rest of the afternoon," he told her. "You can reach me on my cell if something important comes up."

"Okay." There was a slight hesitation. "Is everything all right, Mr. McAvoy?"

"Fine."

In a strange way, it was.

SEVEN

___

Alec was leaning against a lamp-post, finishing up an ice cream cone, when Julia exited the school with a herd of other departing parents. She no longer looked harried. Rather, she was smiling absently, something he'd never seen his own mother do after spending any length of time in his company when he was a kid. Or as an adult for that matter. As hectic as Julia's day had been, it was clear that she'd enjoyed herself.

She saw him and crossed to where he stood.

"You didn't need to wait. I thought I told you that."

"You did. I decided to stick around anyway. I didn't have anything pressing."

She cocked an eyebrow at that, but said nothing. It was out of character for him and they both knew it. He motioned toward the school with the ice cream cone. "So, how did it go?"

The smile was back, more focused this time, when she told him, "It was a lot of fun. The kids acted as servers for the adults. They brought our food to our tables and then took away the dishes afterward."

"Full service."

"Yes. If only I could get them to do that at home without complaining."

"What was on the menu?"

"Deep-fried chicken nuggets—heavy on the breading—French fries and a side salad of iceberg lettuce that came doused in the house dressing, which I think was creamy Italian, although it might have been ranch." Julia wrinkled her nose. "It was hard to tell."

He grimaced on her behalf. "Hungry?"

"I'm starving!" Her laughter bubbled out. "I picked just enough to be polite, but I didn't actually finish anything."

"There's a deli up the block. I could buy you lunch. Repay that debt."

"But you've eaten." She pointed to the ice cream.

"Technically, I haven't. I've only indulged in dessert." He tossed what remained of the cone into the large garbage can that was chained on the opposite side of the lamppost.

"What's the saying? *Life's short. Eat dessert first?* Hmm. I wouldn't have taken you for the sort of person who subscribed to that philosophy."

For the most part, Alec wasn't. He'd made it a point to be the polar opposite of his feckless and free-spirited parents. Still, he said, "You don't know me, Julia. You only know my image—the besmirched one and the one you've been hired to create and replace it with."

"True," she agreed with a slow nod.

"How about we remedy that? Besides, I still have an appetite."

His gaze lowered to her mouth after saying so and he watched her lick her lips. They both were hungry and it went well beyond food. Alec had the advantage and he knew it. He could press and she would buckle, at least momentarily. Then she would spell out the ground rules again. Where was the fun in that? Next move, if there was one, would be hers.

He made the decision, but it didn't stop him from taking her bag from her and then tucking her hand into the crook of his arm. The gesture could be interpreted as merely polite. Old-school manners of the sort his grandfather had complained were sorely lacking among the younger generations. He studied Julia's right hand. Slim fingers were tipped with tidy nails that were painted in clear polish. He'd shed his suit coat out of deference to the heat. He swore he felt his skin tingle through the fabric of his shirt.

They sat in a booth that was snugged up against the windows that faced the street. The spot was prime real estate for people-watching and Julia told Alec as much. He got the impression she would rather keep her gaze trained on the pedestrians wending their way past than let it fall on him for any length of time. Whenever it did, she seemed flustered. His ego took that as a compliment, his libido as a challenge. Regardless, Alec played along. He'd meant it when he'd told Julia that she really didn't know him. Despite some personal details she'd shared with him, he really didn't know her, either. But he wanted to.

"If clothing and body language say so much about a person, tell me about that guy." He pointed to a man clad in black bike shorts and a T-shirt emblazoned with an off-color adjective. His hair was dyed bright green and, thanks to either natural curls or a really bad permanent, it billowed about his head in a frizzy, neon halo.

Instead of answering his question, Julia asked, "Would you hire him to work at Best For Baby?"

"Maybe for the mailroom."

"Image. Fair or not, people make up their minds just that quickly." Julia snapped her fingers. "Now, what if you saw on his resume that he was a Rhodes scholar or graduated top of his class from a prestigious university?"

Alec glanced at the guy again and then shook his head. "It would still be hard to get past the bright hair and offensive T-shirt. That's where you come in, I suppose. What would you do to him?"

"Nothing he wouldn't agree to have done," she remarked dryly.

Alec allowed his grin to show this time. "But you'd exert some pressure, make your preferences known."

The waitress came by with a couple of glasses of ice water and took their orders. A club sandwich for him. Julia went with grilled chicken on a whole wheat bun.

When she was gone, Julia said, "Okay, I'd make my preferences known. But subtly."

"Or not. You know what you want and that's what you go after."

She seemed to consider his assessment before nodding slowly. "I do."

He held up a finger then. "I take that back. I think sometimes, you hold back."

"Of course I do. It's called restraint."

"It's more than that," he challenged.

Her eyes narrowed. "We're not talking about my job now, are we?"

He shook his head. "I want you to get to know the real me. I guess I wouldn't mind if you returned the favor."

"Why?"

"I think you know why."

She reached for her water glass and took a sip.

Alec decided to let that statement sink in for a bit, and returned to the subject they'd been discussing before the waitress's interruption.

"So, back to our guy, suit and tie? Military-style haircut?"

She blinked, and he got the feeling she'd lost her train of thought. It was small of him, but he claimed that as a victory of sorts.

"Oh. Um, it would depend on the kind of job he's after. Creative types have a little more latitude when it comes to their looks and wardrobe."

"I can't think of a position at Best For Baby that has *creative type* in the job description."

"Fine. Then I'd strongly suggest that he lose the hair."

"Shave it?" Alec asked, enjoying himself.

"I was thinking trim it and subdue the color so that it was something a little more natural, but shaving would work, too. Still, long hair doesn't have to be a no-no."

"Do you like long hair on a man?"

She shrugged, but a smile crept into her voice when she said, "I don't mind it on musicians. Take David Lee Roth. I saw some pictures of him where he wore his hair shorter. It looked better long."

"I never would have taken you for a heavy metal groupie."

"Groupie? Please. I'm too old to be a groupie."

"You're what? Thirty?"

"Add a couple years."

"Ancient," he agreed. "Definitely too old to like head-banging music."

"As it happens, my husband played lead guitar in a local band back in the day." She smiled as she shared the information.

"Yeah? Is that how you met?"

"No. We met in chemistry class in the eleventh grade."

"High school sweethearts." Alec whistled through his teeth. He felt strangely envious. The kind of life Julia had led was alien to him, but alluring. His parents, on the other hand, would consider it pedestrian if not downright boring. No jaunts aboard borrowed jets or yachts. No access to private clubs. No butlers or chauffeurs to tend to their needs.

Alec bet that when Julia was a kid, her folks rose at a respectable hour even on the weekends. No lazing abed until well after noon and then starting the day with a cocktail.

"Actually, we weren't high school sweethearts. I thought Scott was a jerk at the time."

That pulled Alec's domestic daydreaming up short. "Yeah?"

"Yeah."

"So much for first impressions."

Her shoulders lifted. "We didn't start to date until a few years after high school graduation. His band played at a little pub near Loyola's campus. He'd outgrown most of his jerkiness by then."

Since it didn't seem to bother her to talk about her late husband, Alec asked, "What was the name of his band?"

"The Grommets." Her laughter was infectious. Alec joined in.

"The Grommets? Seriously?"

"Seriously. And their music was only marginally better than the band's name." She leaned her elbows on the edge of the table and nibbled the inside of her cheek. "In fairness, their cover of The Beach Boys' 'Good Vibrations' was decent."

"The Grommets," Alec said again with a shake of his head. "Am I to assume he didn't go on to make his living as a musician?"

"No. Thank God! He was an accountant."

"With long hair?"

"It was a respectable length by the time he became a CPA, although not quite as short as yours. Anyway, long hair can be attractive, especially if it's kept clean and looks healthy." She tipped her head toward the window. "Even from here I can tell that Mr. Neon's is full of split ends."

"What would you have him wear to, say, an interview for a midlevel executive's job?"

"Well, assuming that is what he's after, I wouldn't automatically put him in a suit and tie."

"No?"

"Some people look so uncomfortable in certain clothes that it defeats the purpose. The idea is for them to put forward the best version of themselves. You don't necessarily want to create a false image."

"That's good to know," he said wryly.

"In your case, it's more a matter of *dispelling* a false image."

"I'm glad you see it that way." He reached for a sugar packet to have something to do with his hands. "I don't think you did at first."

She glanced away before admitting, "I wasn't sure."

"And now?"

"I'm having lunch with you, aren't I?" She flashed a smile, but he wasn't willing to let her off the hook so easily.

"The jury's still out, though. You're not completely convinced."

"I don't know you all that well, Alec."

It was another dodge. Let it go, he told himself. Instead, despite his earlier decision that she would have to make the next move, he called her on it.

"Do you want to get to know me? And I'm not talking about so you can do your job, but because you're interested in, well, dotting the *i*'s and crossing the *t*'s for your own benefit."

"Alec—"

He shook his head, cutting her off.

"Forget it." He wasn't sure why he'd pressed. He wasn't sure what he hoped to accomplish. A date? An affair? When it came to women, he'd always taken the path of least resistance. He chose women who were fun, uncomplicated, fully interested in him. Women who were easy to dismiss when he grew tired of them. And he always grew tired.

He motioned toward the window again. "Let's get back to Mr. Neon Hair. Would you let him wear bike shorts to a job interview?"

"No, but there are a wide range of options to be found between a suit and what one puts on to hang out with friends," she said.

The waitress was back. This time with their glasses of iced tea, a couple of straws and a small plate piled with lemon wedges.

Alec unwrapped a straw. Before putting it in his tea, he used it to point to another man who was perched on a planter box just outside the deli. The guy was wearing olive-green cargo shorts, sneakers and a benign white polo shirt that managed to look dingy even against a backdrop of red geraniums. He was listening to music on an iPod, head bopping in rhythmic fashion.

"Okay, how about that guy? What's your first impression?"

"Well, I'd say comfort is his main priority. The image he projects isn't all that important to him." At Alec's raised brows, she clarified, "His hair is overdue for a trim, he looks as if he hasn't shaved in a couple days and the shorts he's wearing are wrinkled and distressed to the point of fraying around the seams."

"That's the style right now." When her expression registered surprise, he added, "I'm not completely clueless."

"They may be considered fashionable at the moment, but they are still a reflection of the wearer." She smiled. "You wouldn't own a pair of distressed shorts, would you?"

"No."

Her smile turned smug. "I'm guessing that every pair of shorts you own has a crease down the front of the legs that's sharp enough to cut paper."

It was true. "Your point?" he asked dryly.

"You're very...precise, I guess is the word I'm looking for. That's true of more than your appearance. You don't believe in coloring outside the lines."

"Okay, but I might be persuaded otherwise. Under the right circumstances and with the right set of incentives, I can be flexible." At her audible gasp, he frowned. "What?"

"Nothing." She shook her head. "I...it's just an interesting word choice."

"Flexible?"

She pressed her lips together and nodded.

He frowned. "I'm having a hard time deciding if I've just been insulted."

"It's merely an observation."

"Then perhaps it's a good thing we're getting to know one another better, clearing up any lingering misperceptions."

"Perhaps it is."

She fiddled with a packet of sugar, flipping the edge back and forth between her fingers before tearing it open and adding the contents to her tea.

"What are you really thinking, Julia?" he challenged.

"Right now?"

"Right this very minute."

She stirred her tea. "I'm thinking about Danielle and how she has been begging me since Christmas for a pair of jeans that come with holes on the thighs. They take distressed to a new level."

Liar, Alex thought. But he let her off the hook. "And you've said no."

"Repeatedly." Julia's shoulders rose. "Style or not, I can't see plunking down that kind of money on a pair of jeans that will fall apart before she has a chance to outgrow them. Besides, it's nearly summer. She won't be wearing jeans much over the summer."

"That's very practical of you."

"Now I'm not sure if I've been insulted." She grimaced for effect. "Her birthday is coming up. Maybe I'll put a bug in my sister Eloise's ear. The jeans also come in capri length. Danielle could wear them into the fall, even if she has a growth spurt."

"But you just said you didn't think holey jeans were a worthwhile expense?" he reminded her.

She sipped her tea. "The role of mother and cool aunt are different."

"Ah." He squeezed a wedge of lemon into his glass. He couldn't help but be envious. When he was a kid he'd often wished for siblings.

"How many sisters do you have?"

"Just the one."

"And she lives here in Chicago?"

"Just outside the city, actually. She's been after me to move out by her since Scott died. I'd be closer to my parents that way, too."

"So, what's stopping you?"

Julia snorted softly. "A decent down payment. Houses aren't cheap in that area, even with the downturn in the housing market. That's especially true since I'm after something that I won't have to fix up. I don't have time to be handy, even if I owned my own tools, which I don't. So, I'm saving my pennies. I don't want to have a huge mortgage hanging over my head."

Practical, he thought again, but didn't say it. They had very different problems when it came to their housing searches. Alec had plenty of money for a down payment on a turnkey property regardless of price range. He just didn't know what to look for. Julia, on the other hand, appeared to know exactly what she wanted, she just couldn't afford to buy it yet.

"My real estate agent called last night. He has another property he insists is perfect for me."

"Oh? Where is it?" Julia asked.

He rattled off the location, to which Julia let out a wistful sigh.

"That's in an excellent school district."

Which of course would rate high on her wish list.

"My agent told me the same thing." Not that the quality of a school district was important to Alec, except in terms of investment. A home in a well-regarded school district would sell faster and for more money than one in a district whose reputation was not as solid.

"Are you going to see it?" Julia asked.

He hadn't planned to. He'd grown weary of looking, since he wasn't sure what he was looking for. Or even if what he sought existed. An idea formed. Before he had a chance to think it through, he blurted out, "Would you come with me?"

She blinked, every bit as surprised as Alec was that he'd tendered the invitation. But, in a strange way, it made sense. And so he told her, "I'd appreciate the input. It's an investment for me, primarily, but I'm looking for…" He swallowed. His voice sounded hoarse when he admitted, "A home."

"A home," she repeated softly.

The way she was looking at him made Alec feel too exposed. Luckily, the waitress had returned with their sandwiches, saving him from further embarrassment. Or so he thought.

The club sandwich was cut into quarters, each held together with a toothpick spear. He divested one section of its spear and was just getting ready to take a bite when Julia said, "I recall you mentioning that you attended boarding school."

He studied the sandwich, contemplated changing the subject, but he'd told Julia that he wanted to dispel any misconceptions about him she might have. How he was raised said a lot about the man he was—not all of it good. But fair was fair. "From the time I was seven."

"Seven." She pursed her lips. He knew what she was thinking. That was around her kids' ages.

"As I mentioned, my parents led—*lead*," he corrected with a rueful laugh, "a very nomadic lifestyle. That is to say, they enjoy traveling. They have a trip coming up soon, as a matter of fact."

"That couldn't have been easy for you as a child."

"No."

"But you were able to come home for summers and holidays. Right?"

"Generally speaking, children aren't welcome at the places my parents choose to stay." He returned the sandwich to his plate, his appetite waning. He squinted at Julia, "The apple didn't fall far from the tree, huh?"

But she shook her head. "I'm not so sure I believe that anymore," she said, then added, "I'm sorry, Alec. For the boy you were."

Uncomfortable with the sympathy he saw in her eyes, he said, "For the record, when I was a kid, I wouldn't have wanted to tag along with them anyway. Trust me, spending time with a nanny in a hotel suite was even less fun than spending Christmas break at the Albans Preparatory Academy in Connecticut."

Julia only look more looked horrified. "You spent Christmas break at a boarding school? All by yourself? My God! How old were you?"

Which time, Alec thought? He'd awoken on more than one blustery Christmas morning to an empty room in the ivy-covered dormitory before he'd graduated and moved on to college, where, more often than not, he'd done the same. He decided it best not to mention this.

Instead, he said, "I spent some of my Christmases with my grandfather in Nantucket." Four in all. As well as a handful of Easters and summers. "His health wasn't always the best, though."

"I'm sorry, Alec," she said a second time.

He shrugged, his gaze on the sandwich. "It was a long time ago."

"I'm still sorry." This time, she reached across the table and rested a hand on his arm.

Touched by her sincerity, he admitted, "I would like a home of my own, but I don't really know what that means."

"I'm not sure I can help you with that, but I'd be willing to go with you to see the house your agent called about. When would you like to go?"

He was in no hurry and his agent had assured Alec that the house, which had been on the market for more than eight months already, was unlikely to be snapped up anytime soon. "I was thinking I'd wait until the weekend. Saturday? Whatever time works best for you."

"I've got a few hours free in the early afternoon."

"Are you sure you don't mind?"

She picked up the paper napkin that was folded under her cutlery and spread it over her lap. He half expected her to qualify her agreement by relating it to work. In truth, he was almost hoping she would. That way he would have felt less nervous and exposed.

But all she said was, "I'm sure."

EIGHT

——

The rest of the week passed in a blur for Julia, as she crammed end-of-the-school-year activities into her already packed daytime routine. Not only had she managed to slip away from the office for Colin's field day and Danielle's awards assembly, but she'd also dropped off cookies for a PTO fund-raiser and, as the first-grade homeroom mom, she'd collected money from the other parents to purchase a gift for the teacher.

To accomplish all of this and stay on top of everything at the office, she'd burned the midnight oil after putting her kids to bed. To stay awake and energized, she'd been making her morning coffee so strong that the spoon all but stood up in it.

By the time the weekend rolled around, she was exhausted and a little amazed that she'd managed to cross so many things off both her personal and professional to-do lists.

Overall, she was pleased with the progress she was making on Alec's revamped image. He was still being bashed in cyberspace, but not quite as badly. As anticipated, the television interview with the mom from the park had been pure gold, especially since the network had picked it up and the story had gone national. The good press only added to how well he'd done on the other programs she'd booked for him. It hadn't scored the kind of reach that Alec's initial article had garnered, but it was making the rounds on the internet and being talked about on blogs, including the one Alec had taken a guest turn on just the day before.

His carefully crafted guest entry, which Julia had gone over with a fine-toothed comb before allowing him to submit it, was getting a lot of hits.

She logged on to her computer and checked the comments again early Saturday morning as she sat in her tidy home office wearing yoga clothes and sipping green tea. Julia had decided to switch to a lower-octane caffeine beverage after her mother remarked at the previous evening's soccer match that Julia was talking faster than an auctioneer.

She scrolled down to the end of the article, where more than six hundred comments had been left. They were a mixed bag. Some were filled with vitriol. Others made it clear the poster was at least willing to give Alec the benefit of the doubt, with a smattering of messages firmly in his camp. Taken in total, they represented a major shift from previous blogs, where the comments easily had run ninety percent against him.

Julia was pleased, but she'd been in the perception business long enough to know better than to declare victory. She equated the progress made during the past week to drips of water. A few drips didn't do much. But enough of them, pounding down in relentless succession, could alter the landscape.

Were they enough to save Alec's job? It was too early to tell what impact her efforts were having on stockholders' perceptions and the company's bottom line. The bigger question in Julia's mind had become: Were her efforts enough to save Alec?

Like the public at large, her opinion of him was shifting, with her emotions threatening to catch up to the physical attraction that had been there from the start. A lot of what she saw, she liked. And some of what she now understood about his character made her ache for him. Christmases alone? School breaks spent in empty dormitories or in the care of nannies? An aging grandfather who had tried to fill the gaps, but couldn't because of health issues?

Was it any wonder Alec wasn't sure what a real home was supposed to feel like?

Or that family life was a mystery to him? He saw children as an inconvenience because that was what he had been to his parents. More amazing to Julia was that he wasn't more emotionally stunted.

Unfortunately, not everyone shared her view, Julia noted as she continued to skim the blog entries.

THE MAN IS A MONSTER!!!! one read. It was hard to skip over since it relied so heavily on capital letters and exclamation points. HE SHOULDN'T BE ALLOWED AROUND KIDS, MUCH LESS RUNNING A COMPANY DEDICATED TO THEM. DON'T LET THE PR CAMPAIGN FOOL YOU!!!!

She frowned at the "shouted" comment, her stomach knotting, until she came to the next one. And the next. And the one after that. Three readers in swift succession had rallied to his defense. And so it went, back and forth, but with comments generally running in his favor. Her brows hitched up when she came to a few, presumably written by single moms, in which the commenter offered to "help" Alec get over his aversion to children. The phone rang as Julia read one of those.

Alec's voice greeted her, eliciting a shiver. She told herself it was his timing rather than the pleasing tenor of his voice that caused it.

"I hope I'm not disturbing you," he began. "I took the chance that you'd be up since it's nearly nine. And, well, kids, they get up early. Right?"

"Since seven," she agreed. Julia had risen an hour before them out of habit, even though she hadn't called it a night until just after one. Danielle and Colin were watching cartoons in the living room. They'd eaten breakfast and were dressed. "What are you wearing... doing?" She frowned at the Freudian slip. Before he could reply, she added, "I'm reading the blog comments. More than six hundred have been left so far."

Rather than sounding impressed, Alec sighed. "You work too hard."

"This from the man who spends his Saturdays at the office?" She wound the telephone cord around her index finger as she said it. Both the extension in the kitchen and the one in her bedroom were cordless. When the power went out, so did her connection, so she kept one with a cord. It didn't hurt that it was red and retro-looking.

"You've reformed me. As it happens, I'm sitting on the rooftop deck of my apartment right now, having my morning coffee. Nothing but blue water and blue sky as far as the eye can see. It's going to be a beautiful day."

She glanced out her window at the brick façade of the building across the street. He definitely had her beat when it came to the view.

"Want to know what they're saying about you?" she asked.

"Only if it's good."

"Depends on your definition of good. JuniorJumper thinks you're hot and MightyMom214 wants to know if you're seeing anyone. She'd like to go on a date."

"MightyMom214, hmm? Does she look like my type?"

His type? What exactly was Alec's type? A mere week ago Julia would have been sure she knew. Her gaze returned to the computer screen. "It's hard to say. Her avatar is Rosie the Riveter. Does that help?"

The laughter echoing through the receiver was warm and inviting. "It doesn't hurt. I like strong women."

Julia leaned back in her chair. "Do you now?"

"As long as they can't beat me at arm wrestling, what's not to like?"

"I'm having a hard time picturing you arm wrestling with anyone, male or female."

"I think I've just been insulted."

Their easy banter was new, having evolved over the past few days. Alec had begun calling Julia just after 10:00 p.m. Her kids were in bed by then and the two of them used the time to fine-tune plans for the following day. At least that was how the phone calls had started. More and more, they were social in nature. Hence the banter. She liked it, but it made her nervous for reasons she wasn't quite brave enough to investigate.

"I wouldn't dream of insulting a client. That would be unprofessional of me."

A thick slice of silence hung between them after Julia's intentional reminder of the exact nature of their relationship.

His reply, when it came, was lighthearted. Still, it jabbed at her conscience.

"Client, hmm? And here I thought we were becoming friends."

"We're that, too."

"For now," it sounded like he said. Then, "Do you still have time to go with me to see the house today? I can make an appointment for two o'clock if that works. If you're busy…"

His words trailed off. He was giving her an out and they both knew it. A smart woman, especially a businesswoman, would have played it safe and taken it, no matter how much she wanted to help Alec. Julia considered herself to be smart. She didn't take unnecessary risks. She had too much to lose.

But she said, "I'm not too busy. Besides, I'm curious about the house."

Her conscience called her a liar after she hung up. Julia was curious about far more than the house.

Julia's building was a squat, redbrick rectangle that took up half a block in a mostly residential neighborhood. It was located within walking distance from an

"L" train stop and a small park, and just two streets over was a market and a smattering of retail shops. Alec had to circle the block three times before he found an open parking spot. He recognized Julia's car three vehicles up from his. Apparently, she'd gotten it back from the shop. She'd been driving a loaner—a minivan—for the past few days. He'd been a little concerned she might suggest he trade in his Porsche so he could be seen tooling about town in one of those family-friendly vehicles.

After setting the alarm on his car, he headed for the entrance. Her building didn't have a security guard or a lobby, for that matter, so he stood on the covered stoop and pressed her apartment number, then had to wait to be buzzed inside. Her apartment was on the third floor. The building had no elevator. The stairs were made of cement. He took them two at a time. The door to 3B was adorned with a wreath made of multicolored handprints. Two pairs of rain boots—one sporting green dinosaurs and the other pink leopard spots—sat beside the welcome mat. The door opened before Alec had a chance to knock. Colin grinned up at him.

"Hi, Mr. McAvoy. Mom said to tell you to come in. She's almost ready."

Though Alec's shoes were clean, he wiped his feet on the welcome mat before stepping side.

"You can call me Alec, if you'd like," he told Colin.

"Okay." Then the little boy wrinkled his nose. "You have a funny name."

Intrigued rather than insulted, Alec asked, "How so?"

"Whenever I talk back, my mom says I'm being a smart aleck."

Alec pretended to give the boy's comment serious consideration, even though it was hard to keep his laughter from spilling out. "I see what you mean."

"Awkward," Colin said soberly.

Exactly. But growing less so, Alec mused. Maybe it was because he saw so much of Julia in the boy's round face.

A small hallway that apparently doubled as a foyer led to the living room. What the space lacked in size it made up for in charm. On the far wall, books and bric-a-brac lined shelves on either side of a tastefully sized, flat-screen television. A ballgame was on. The Cubs were playing and winning from the looks of it. The announcer's voice was steady and almost hypnotic as he recounted a recent play at third base.

Home, Alec thought. This was just such a place. It exuded the personality and warmth his apartment lacked. It was small, but so welcoming, warm and inviting, filled as it was with comforting sounds and scents.

He turned then and spied an older man sitting in an overstuffed chair in the corner. The man stood and stepped forward, meeting Alec at the center of the room, where they shook hands.

"I'm Alec McAvoy."

"Lyle Bellamy, Julia's dad."

A surprising amount of trepidation skittered up Alec's spine, and he actually had to clear his throat before he could say, "It's nice to meet you."

Lyle nodded, but rather than returning the sentiment, he said, "Colin, why don't you see what your mom is up to." He waited until they were alone to continue. "Julia has told me a little bit about you."

It was a good thing this wasn't a date or Alec figured he would be in trouble. He could tell from the way her father was sizing him up that he'd been found lacking.

"Oh? What has she said?"

"She mentioned that you have a rather serious public relations dilemma."

Work. Of course. "That I do."

"I've read all about your...gaffe." It was a diplomatic description, and they both knew it. "I can see why you need her."

"I'm hoping she can turn my fortunes around."

"Count on it. She's very good at her job." This was said with no small amount of pride.

"That's why my company's board of directors hired her." A move Alec had resented at the time. He'd since changed his tune, for reasons more complicated than the shifting sands of public opinion.

"She can make anyone believe anything when it comes to her clients." The older man stepped a closer. "Sometimes I worry that she might lose objectivity and start to believe her own spin."

Several beats of silence followed.

"I can see why you would find that troubling," Alec said at last.

"She's been through a lot."

Alec cleared his throat again. "I know about her husband. I'm sorry for your loss as well."

Lyle acknowledged this with a curt nod. "Scott was everything a father hopes for in the man his daughter chooses to marry. She hasn't dated much since he died. In fact, I haven't had the chance to meet any of the men she's been out with."

"Oh, um, is that so?"

Alec felt heat creep into his cheeks. He wasn't sure what else to say. He could deny he and Julia were seeing one another. They weren't. Were they?

Julia cleared up the matter with a disturbing amount of conviction. "Alec and I aren't going on a date."

She stood under the archway that led from what Alec assumed was the kitchen. A woman was next to her. She was an older version of Julia, with shorter, darker hair that was streaked with silver.

"Lyle!" the older woman admonished. Then she said, "I'm Sherry Bellamy. Julia's mom."

"My mistake," Lyle said, offering an affable smile that didn't fool anyone.

"He's retired," Sherry said, as if that explained everything. To Lyle she added, "You need to get a hobby and keep your nose out of Julia's business."

Lyle shrugged. "It's just that I can't recall another time Julia spent a Saturday with a client that didn't involve, well, business. She said they are going to look at houses."

This time, it was Julia who flushed.

"House, Dad. Singular. And I'm simply doing Alec a favor. Like you and Mom are doing me a favor by watching the kids." She crossed to where her father stood and rose on tiptoe to kiss his leathery cheek. "Alec and I shouldn't be gone long. A couple of hours tops."

He grunted. "So, you'll be back in time for the five of us to make a matinee show this afternoon?"

"Of course I will. This won't take all day."

After kissing her children goodbye and reminding them to be on their best behavior, Julia and Alec were on their way.

"Sorry about my dad," she said once they were seated in his car.

"No need to apologize. It's kind of nice how he's still looking out for you."

She chuckled. "I'm glad you see it that way."

"So, you haven't dated much?"

She fidgeted with her hands. "No."

He reached over, took one in his. "Why is that? I can't believe it's for lack of offers."

As compliments went, it was pretty benign. Still, her heart thunked out an extra beat. Maybe it was because of that extra beat that she sought to remind them both of reality. "I've gone on some dates. Mostly first dates that don't lead to a second."

Again, he asked why and she slid him a look. "I think you know why. I'm part of a package, Alec."

"Your kids."

Julia nodded. "Not many men are interested in a single mom, as I'm sure you can understand."

Alec returned his attention to the road. She expected him to release her hand, but he didn't. His fingers remained twined through hers for the rest of the drive.

The house they were going to see was half an hour outside the city in an established neighborhood, where lots were generously proportioned and lawns impeccably manicured. Julia knew without asking that the prices would be well beyond her range, even once she'd saved up a sizeable down payment. Still, she gave a wistful sigh as they drove down the tree-lined street.

"What?" Alec asked.

"It's a great neighborhood. Very quiet and secure-feeling." Children could ride their bikes here or play outside without constant adult supervision. It was exactly what she wanted for Danielle and Colin. Not to mention that her commute to work in the city would be reasonable. "And the school district has an excellent art program. A lot of schools, especially public ones, have cut back on their art programs in recent years. But not this one. I'd love to be able to send Danielle here."

"She's into art?"

Julia nodded. "Into it and very good at it. She wants to go to an art camp in August."

"Have you signed her up?"

"I...no."

"What's stopping you? If you don't mind my asking."

"It's an hour away and lasts a full week, for starters. She's only nine. She's never been away from home for more than a night, and then only with my parents or sister."

"I already had two years of boarding school under my belt by that time."

"Were you afraid the first time you had to stay away from your family overnight?"

"Afraid? No." He was quiet a moment. "More like confused. I thought I'd done something wrong, especially when my friends went home on weekends and I stayed there."

"That must have been lonely."

"It was." He angled her a look. "I took a pair of scissors one weekend when I was in the second grade and cut up all of my uniforms. I figured I would be in big trouble and my parents would have to come for me."

She didn't need to consult Dr. Spock to know that from a kid's point of view, bad attention was better than no attention at all.

"Did they?" she asked.

"No. They paid for new uniforms. So, I did it again. And again, which wasn't easy, since my scissors had been confiscated." This time, he winked. "The law of supply and demand applied. I offered one of the kids in my class my desserts for a month if he'd smuggle me in a new pair. He did. After the third offense, the school expelled me."

"And your parents finally showed up," Julia guessed, struggling to hold back her outrage.

"No. But they sent a driver, who took me to my grandfather. I stayed there for a week before I was enrolled in another school. The Borden-Sandville Academy for Boys. The uniform shirts were forest-green." His lip curled.

"Hence your aversion to that color."

"Exactly." Alec pulled the car up a long, curved driveway and parked behind a sedan. "This is it."

A middle-aged man was leaning against the sedan. He was wearing a suit. The smile on his face was hopeful. Alec's real estate agent, no doubt. Julia's gaze didn't stay on the Realtor long. It went to the house. It was easily the largest one on the street. It was two stories with tall, arched windows, a carved wood front door and a stacked stone-and-stucco façade. Impressive. Imposing.

"Wow," Julia said.

Alec switched off the car's engine and jiggled the keys in his hand. "Is that good wow or bad wow?"

She wasn't sure. The house was beautiful. No doubt about that. But was it a home? That was hard to say without going inside.

"Just wow for now."

"Alec, good to see you." The real estate agent clamped Alec's hand and gave it an enthusiastic pumping when they reached him. "Nice place, isn't it?"

"You haven't taken me to see a listing that hasn't been nice, Fred," Alec admitted.

Afterward, he made the introductions. Julia pretended not to notice the speculation brewing in Fred Owens's eyes.

"Let's go inside. You're going to love it," the agent said enthusiastically.

They toured the main floor first. The house had been built in the 1950s and then totally renovated half a decade before. Walls had been removed to enlarge the kitchen. The finishes there were top-of-the-line: granite, tumbled marble, polished hardwoods. The appliances were a chef's dream. But it felt cold to Julia. It felt soulless.

That impression continued in the formal dining room, which boasted a table large enough to seat ten people. The wood was dark and intricately carved. Ornate.

"It's very…spacious," Julia said when Alec turned to her, eyebrows raised as if to say, *Well?*

Her words were whispered. This was a room where conversations would be carried out in hushed tones rather than in the animated, higher-decibel free-for-alls Julia's family engaged in whenever they gathered around her parents' table to share holiday meals.

"You don't like it," Alec said.

"It's not that I don't like it, it's just not my taste. But then, I'm not one for fancy dinner parties. In your line of work, I would imagine you probably attend them and, with a room like this, would host some."

He grimaced, but nodded thoughtfully. They moved on to the great room. It also had a formal feel, furnished as it was in traditional pieces with classical art decorating the walls.

"The fireplace is gas," the agent said.

He picked up a remote from the mantel and with the push of a button, flames leapt behind the glass in the hearth. The room still lacked warmth, Julia thought.

After that they toured a wood-paneled den furnished in heavy, masculine pieces and a sunroom outfitted in brown wicker chairs and a settee, before heading upstairs. The second story had four bedrooms, each with its own bathroom. The master was at the end of the hallway on the other side of a pair of double doors. Just as Fred opened them, his cell phone chirped.

"Go on in and take a look around," he said. "I'll answer this and catch up with you."

Alec's hand was on the small of her back, urging her

forward. Once they were inside, he kept it there. Julia tried to ignore the warmth radiating from it.

"I think this may be the size of my entire apartment," she commented.

Even with the current owners' king-sized four-poster taking up a notable chunk of square footage, the room was large enough to accommodate a separate sitting area with its own fireplace. The big bed drew her gaze. She told herself it was because she would like a bed that size in her apartment, if only she had the space. Maybe then when the kids sneaked into her full-sized one at night, as they often did, she wouldn't wake up with a stiff neck from sleeping in an awkward position. Yes, that's why she was fixated on the bed.

She glanced at Alec. His gaze was on the bed, too, before it cut back to her. His eyes turned smoky. Julia was no longer picturing her children with her in the bed then, and the hand at her back no longer felt relaxed, friendly. The palm that had been resting flat curved and she felt his fingers dig in, clutching the fabric of her shirt. He turned to face her. She took a step closer, urged nearer by the pressure at her back. She was wearing flat shoes, giving him the advantage of height. She had no choice but to look up. Their gazes caught and held for that brief moment, before their mouths met.

"Mmm." The sound hummed from the back of her throat as her arms came up to ring his neck. Not for a moment did she consider backing away.

"Julia." He whispered her name as his lips left hers and found the sensitive spot on her neck just below her ear. His hands moved, too, from the safety of her back down to her hips and then over the curve of her bottom.

Time, place, propriety—all were forgotten. She pressed her body flush to his, moaning a second time as her soft curves yielded to his hard angles.

A discreet cough sounded from the doorway. They jumped apart.

"The, uh, ceiling is a nice feature in this room," the real estate agent said in a strained voice.

Julia wanted to be mortified. But that wasn't *all* she wanted to be. Her gaze fell on the bed, before moving to Alec. One side of his mouth rose in what she took to be a frustrated smile. They both looked up then, at the ceiling in question, a multilevel tray that was accented with crown molding and painted in complementing shades. She concentrated on the chandelier that hung in the center, and willed her breathing back to normal.

"The house boasts excellent craftsmanship and décor throughout, which you would, of course, expect at this price point," Fred was saying. "In fact, I think the owners will be willing to come down on asking if you're interested. The husband has already relocated across the country for his job. His wife stayed behind to see to the sale. As I mentioned, the house has been on the market now for several months."

"Something to think about," Alec murmured. His gaze cut from the ceiling to Julia before he crossed to a pair of French doors that led to the balcony. He stepped outside.

Alec needed fresh air and a moment to compose himself. The house, even at a lower price, didn't move him to make an offer. But he'd felt *something* in the bedroom with Julia. It wasn't that sense of home he was seeking. No. Nothing quite that comfortable. Indeed, his current condition was making him downright *uncomfortable*. He wasn't sure whether to be glad or not that his agent was present, cast in the inadvertent role of chaperone. One thing he knew for certain, he wanted Julia in a way he couldn't recall ever wanting another woman, and that made him nervous.

He heard the door creak behind him as Fred and Julia joined him on the balcony. It was large enough to accommodate a bistro set and a lounge chair, but it felt crowded with the three of them.

"It's a lovely yard," Julia remarked. He wondered if she was looking out at it to avoid looking at him.

"Even with no swing set?" Alec asked, consciously inserting her children into the conversation, even though he wasn't quite sure why he wanted them there.

"There's certainly enough room for one," the agent remarked.

Julia said nothing. Absently, she plucked a dead bloom from the brightly colored annuals that spilled from the planter box attached to the rail.

Fred continued, "The lot measures nearly an acre. The current owners retain the services of a local landscaping company to oversee maintenance."

Alec glanced back out over the yard again, trying to picture swings and a slide. But he couldn't get beyond the water feature and koi pond or the immaculately groomed lawn. It looked like a miniature park or... He frowned.

"It reminds me of the campus of the school I attended as a boy. Pretty and polished, but not exactly where I want to spend my time just the same."

Julia's grimace telegraphed her sympathy.

Fred cleared his throat. "I'll leave you alone to discuss this with your, um, friend."

When they were alone, Alec leaned against the balcony's wrought-iron railing. "I suppose this is where you remind me of our professional relationship and tell me that we shouldn't kiss like that again."

"Is that what I'm supposed to do?" From Julia's smile, he couldn't be sure if she was mocking him or making fun of herself.

"You have other ideas?"

She waited a couple of agonizing heartbeats before shaking her head slowly. "No. You're right. Or, would I be the one who's right, since you already gave me credit for making the decision?"

"You're a smart woman. So, that's the end of it then." He smiled.

"I'd like to think so."

"But you know better." A minute ago, he hadn't felt like smiling. Now, he did.

"Alec—"

"Let's drop it for now." He crossed his arms, in part to ward off temptation, and changed the subject. "So what do you think about the house? Give me your honest opinion."

Julia looked relieved to have something other than their mutual attraction to discuss.

"It's nice," she began. "So much space for entertaining and, as your agent pointed out, the finishes are first-rate."

"But it's not a home," he observed with a shake of his head. He'd reached that conclusion on his own already.

"I...no. It doesn't feel that way to me. I like the neighborhood, but the house... It looks like something you'd see in a magazine. Too...staged. It's picture perfect, but not the sort of place where people actually live or spend any amount of time."

"It has no soul," he agreed.

Julia blinked. "That was exactly my thought as we walked through it. Sorry, Alec."

She put her hand on his arm in commiseration only to pull it away and take a step back.

"Don't trust me?" he asked softly.

"I don't trust either of us."

Her unflagging honesty was going to be his undoing, he decided, on a barely audible oath.

They returned downstairs. Fred was in the kitchen, his expression hopeful.

"Another bust, I'm afraid," Alec told him.

The older man sighed and nodded. "I had a feeling that was what you were going to say."

"Sorry to waste more of your time."

Fred shrugged. "I'll go through the listings again first thing on Monday. Your home is out there, Alec. We'll find it eventually."

The agent said the same thing after every showing. Alec glanced at Julia. For the first time, he thought maybe Fred was right.

NINE

—

Another week passed. Julia's kids were officially out of school. That meant St. Augustine's summer program for them three days of the week. The other two, she bundled them off to her parents' house, where they spent time playing with their cousins. It was a good arrangement, all things considered, even if her Thursdays and Fridays would be a little more hectic because of the added drive time. Her parents told her she could leave the kids with them overnight on Thursdays.

"It would give you a little break," her mother said after the making the offer again during a phone conversation. "You could go out with your girlfriends."

"I'll think about it," Julia said, not bothering to point out that most of her friends were married and had kids of their own. Their free time was at a premium, too.

"Or you could go out with Alec. He seemed like a nice enough young man," Sherry added slyly. So much for admonishing her husband to stay out of their daughter's business. "And so handsome."

Julia had smiled weakly before saying once again, "I'll think about it."

Indeed, she did. Alec was on her mind constantly. Of course, her campaign to revitalize and revamp his image was in full swing, so it made sense that he was front and center in her thoughts.

She'd planted dozens of stories in publications around the country, sent out scores of tweets on Twitter, and had set up several appearances in and around Chicago, including a very high-profile one at the upcoming Midwest Family Fun Expo. The annual event was a huge draw for mothers, and was slated for that Thursday through Saturday in the grand ballroom of one of Chicago's most posh hotels. Best For Baby was already a gold-level sponsor. Thanks to another hefty donation, it had gone platinum and Julia had wrangled Alec a stint in an on-stage demonstration called Cooking with Kids.

The good news was that the segment would be aired on television. The not-so-good news was that it would air live. That meant no editing. Whatever Alec did or said would be out there for mass consumption. One wrong move, one verbal faux pas, and they would be back at square one as far as his image was concerned.

She told him as much when she swung by his office just before noon on Monday.

"Cooking with Kids, hmm? What exactly will I be doing?"

"Exactly what it sounds like. You will be cooking with kids."

His eyes narrowed. "Whose kids? Am I supposed to bring some with me or will they be provided in much the same way the pots and pans and utensils will be?"

Julia shook her head at his glib remark. "The other celebrity chefs in the segment will have children with them, in most cases their own. In your case, we'll send out a memo to Best For Baby's staff, seeking volunteers. A number of your employees will be at the expo anyway. It will be painless," she assured him.

He didn't share her confidence. "I don't know," he said slowly. "Couldn't I be a celebrity taster or something like that?"

"No. The segment calls for chefs. The audience will be doing the tasting." She swallowed. "You know how to cook, right? I'm talking the basics here, like fry an egg and flip a hamburger."

"It's a little late to be asking, isn't it? You've already signed me up."

Julia stomach contracted. "Do you? Please tell me you do."

"I think I could bring water to a boil if I had to." His expression brightened. "And I know my way around the microwave. Well, as long as it involves hitting the reheat-entree button."

He wasn't kidding. "Oh, God!" She slumped back in her seat.

She'd seen the kitchen in his apartment. It was gorgeous. Sure, Alec was a bachelor and had grown up in privilege. Still, she'd assumed, foolishly as it turned out, that he would have a rudimentary knowledge of meal preparation. Who didn't know how to fry an egg, for goodness sake?

"Do you eat out *every* night?" she asked.

"Not *out* necessarily. I'm often still at my office at dinnertime. It's easier to have meals delivered. The side benefit is there are no dishes to wash afterward."

He smiled. She didn't.

"That's not healthy, Alec." Not to mention it had to be expensive. And lonely. So very lonely.

"I have an arrangement with the chefs at a couple of nearby restaurants. They prepare lower-fat, lower-sodium versions of menu favorites for me." He shrugged. "It costs a little more, but, given my schedule, it makes more sense than having a personal chef cooking meals in my apartment."

Julia made a quick decision.

"Tonight, you'll come to my apartment for dinner." She still didn't trust either of them. Their attraction was nearing the combustible range at times. But they would have a couple of watchful chaperones. What could happen with her kids underfoot? "Does six o'clock work for you?"

"Julia, you don't have to make dinner for me."

"Oh, I'm not. You'll be the one wearing the apron," she added with a grin. "Clearly, you need some practice before your culinary debut."

His brows shot up and she thought he might object. But he asked, "What am I making?"

"We'll keep it simple."

"Mac and cheese? I hear it comes in a box with the directions printed on the side." His lips twitched with a smile.

"Not *that* simple." She stood and smiled in return.

"Be on time, please. The natives get restless if they have to wait too long to be fed."

She expected that news to cause his grin to slip. Instead, he smiled wider. His voice was a seductive whisper when he taunted, "Does that include you?"

"This isn't a social call, is it?" Julia said ten minutes into a chat with her sister that afternoon.

"That obvious? Shoot! I was trying for subtle."

Eloise had started hinting around about Julia's love life right after the hellos were out of the way. So much for subtle.

"Did Mom put you up to it?"

"Actually, Dad. When I stopped over at the house last night, he said there was a new man in your life. I was surprised and a little miffed, I might add, that you hadn't mentioned anything to me."

"There's nothing to mention. Alec's a client."

"Uh-huh." Her sister sounded as convinced as Julia felt. "Dad told me that, too. That's what has him worried, Jul. He said the two of you went house-hunting."

"Oh, good grief! We didn't go house-hunting. We went to look at a house—singular—that Alec was considering buying. He lives in an apartment and he wanted my opinion. That's all."

But it wasn't *all*. Not by a long shot. She touched her lips, felt the tingle of need and bit back a sigh.

On the other end of the line, Eloise was saying, "Dad looked him up online while I was over. He's gorgeous."

"His picture doesn't do him justice," she admitted.

"Are you attracted to him?"

Irritated with both of them, Julia snapped, "Of

course, I'm attracted to him. You just said yourself he's gorgeous. I'm a single mother. I'm not a nun."

"Okaaay."

"Sorry."

"Want to talk about it?"

"Actually, El, I don't even want to *think* about it. But thanks."

"Just be careful."

"I'm always careful."

Too much was at stake to be anything but. Still, a forgotten part of herself was rising up, threatening to rebel. The question keeping her awake at night was: Would she let it?

Alec caught himself glancing at the clock all afternoon. He needed to be on time. It had nothing to do with being eager. Still, anticipation was what he felt as he drove away from the Best For Baby offices just after five o'clock. He stopped at a corner market on the way to Julia's. He selected a bottle of red wine first, put it back on the shelf and opted for white. He put that one back, too. Wine with a weeknight meal that Julia had assured him would be basic seemed too formal. Maybe even presumptuous. For all he knew, she didn't drink. He stopped in the soda aisle and decided Julia wouldn't appreciate him plying Danielle and Colin with sugar and empty calories, even if it probably would score him points with her kids. And, he could admit, he was nervous about spending an evening with them.

Since it seemed wrong to show up empty-handed, he selected a bouquet of daisies from the bin by the register.

"Will that be all?" the woman at the checkout asked.

The flowers were for Julia, but what about the kids? Shouldn't he bring something for them?

"Well?" the woman prompted.

He glanced at the array of impulse purchases set out in front of him and grabbed two battery-powered miniature fans. "I'll take these as well."

This time, it was Danielle who opened the door when he arrived at the apartment. The little girl didn't look happy to see him.

"Hi, Danielle."

"Hello." She didn't step to one side to allow him to enter. The keeper of the gate, he thought.

"How's soccer going?"

"Good."

Colin joined them then.

"Hi...*Alec*." The little boy fell into a fit of giggles. No doubt, he was thinking *Smart Aleck*.

"Hi."

They were both staring at him now. Alec would rather be facing his board of directors.

"Your mom's here, right?"

"Yep," Colin said. "She's changing her clothes."

Alec glanced toward a hallway that he assumed led to the bedrooms. If the image that popped into his mind were a movie, it would have been rated R. Definitely not appropriate for children. He forced it away.

"Um, would it be all right if I came in?"

Were the decision left to Danielle, he had the feeling he would have remained out in the hall. But Colin grabbed his arm.

"Sure."

Alec wiped his feet on the doormat and followed them into the living room, where he took a seat on the couch. The flowers and plastic bag were grasped in his hands, and even though he was resting one ankle on the opposite leg's knee, he was far from relaxed. The television was on. Cartoons were playing. But both Colin and Danielle were watching him rather than the TV screen. Oh, yeah, he would definitely rather be facing his board of directors.

He attempted to swallow around a knot of nerves and asked, "How was school today?"

"We're out of school," Danielle replied with a roll of her eyes.

"It's summer vacation," Colin reminded him.

"Oh. Right. Summer vacation."

"They had those even back when you were a kid, right?" the boy asked.

"Yes. Even *waaaay* back then," Alec replied dryly. "So, what did the two of you do all day?"

"We went to St. Augustine," Danielle said on a sigh.

"That's our school. A lot of kids go there during the summer while their parents are at work. We don't have to do any school work or anything," Colin added. "Mostly, we just play with our friends, and sometimes we take field trips. Next week, we're going to a museum."

"Oh."

His expression must have soured because Colin said, "Did you have to do that in the summer when you were a kid, too?"

"Sort of, except I was there around the clock."

"You lived there?" Danielle's appalled expression

was a twin of her mother's. Maybe that was why he found it so endearing.

"I attended a boarding school. So, yeah, I lived there."

"Tough break," Colin said with a shake of his head. "In the summer, we only have to go to St. Augustine on Mondays, Tuesdays and Wednesdays, and even then only for part of the day. We're always home for dinner."

"What do you do on Thursdays and Fridays?" Alec asked.

"Mom takes us to Grandma and Grandpa Bellamy's house. It's out in 'burbia."

"*Su*burbia," Danielle corrected with another roll of her eyes.

"That sounds like fun."

"Grandpa lets us eat raw cookie dough," Colin confided.

"Colin!" Danielle gasped.

"We're not supposed to tell anyone," the little boy said. "You're not going to say anything to our mom, are you?"

"Who? Me? I can keep a secret."

Julia emerged from the hallway right then. She was wearing a pair of khaki shorts that ended at midthigh and a white T-shirt with a scooped neckline. Even though the outfit covered everything, his imagination began filling in the blanks. He bit back a groan and willed his thoughts to stay in the PG range, given their audience. The woman had a first-rate pair of legs. Pale, since she didn't have a lot of time to spend sunning herself outdoors and apparently didn't bother with a faux tan. But they were slim and shapely. An image of those legs wrapped around Alec's waist worked its way past his best intentions.

"What's this about secrets?" she asked.

Alec had a few he wouldn't have minded sharing if they were alone. He glanced at Colin and Danielle. Their eyes were wide, as if they expected him to rat them out about the raw cookie dough. He rose to his feet and handed Julia the flowers instead.

"I hope you like daisies."

Julia's face flushed with pleasure. "What's not to like about daisies? Thank you."

Colin came over and gave them a sniff. He wrinkled his nose afterward and declared, "They kinda stink."

"They don't stink." Julia looked horrified.

Alec leaned over and inhaled. His gaze held hers. "They don't really have much of a smell," he said diplomatically.

A smile tugged at the corners of her mouth. If they were alone, Alec would have given in to temptation and kissed her. He probably should be happy for their audience, he thought, since it was keeping him from doing something that neither of them was sure was wise.

"What's in the bag?" Colin asked.

"These are for you and Danielle." Now that he was handing them over, Alec felt embarrassed. "They're not much. Just something that caught my eye while I was standing at the register."

"Cool! Little fans!" Colin shouted. He had the plastic blades of his whirling around even before Danielle had hers out of the bag.

"I, um, don't think they can cause injury," Alec told Julia. At least he hoped.

Colin put his index finger to the blade to test out the theory. The fan slapped at it and then stopped until he pulled it away.

"Nope. No blood. And it hardly hurt at all, Mom."

Alec smiled weakly. "It was these or candy," he said to Julia.

"Then I appreciate your restraint." To her children she said, "What do you say to Mr. McAvoy?"

"Thank you," they replied in unison. Then Colin said, "He said I can call him Alec."

Giggles ensued. Julia cut a questioning gaze to Alec, who shrugged.

"Come on," Julia said, rolling her eyes. "Let's go start dinner."

They left the kids in the living room, playing with the fans and watching television. Her kitchen was small, but like the rest of the apartment, it was tidy. Four places were already set at the table. Julia arranged the flowers in a vase and put them in the center. The arrangement was simple, the perfect complement to the basic white dishes and folded paper napkins. Alec often ate off fine china and dabbed his mouth with Irish linen. Yet he doubted he'd ever seen anything more perfect.

Home.

"Something wrong?" she asked.

"No." He shook his head as the word echoed in his head. "No," he said again. "So, what are we making?"

"First things first."

She opened a drawer and held out a white chef's apron. It had *Kiss the Cook* written across the bib. He cocked an eyebrow up at that and thought, why not?

He intended the kiss to be light, friendly. More than the sort of kiss a man would give his mother, but short of the sort he would give a lover. It was brief and reasonably chaste. But nothing about it was friendly.

She stared at him afterward, her fingers touching her lips. "What was that for?"

"Just following instructions," he managed to respond in a casual tone as he pointed to the slogan on the apron she still held.

She blinked, visibly off-kilter. "But I'm not the cook."

"Then I guess you should be kissing me."

"Alec—"

"It's just a kiss. Chicken?" He wondered if she'd take the dare.

She glanced toward the doorway. Debating?

"Why don't you take off your coat and tie." The request had his full attention until she added, "And roll up your shirt sleeves."

Ah. Right. Even wearing an apron, it wouldn't be a good idea to prepare a meal in a tailored suit. He made a soft clucking sound as he began to peel off the jacket. Her eyes narrowed. His arms were tangled in gabardine when she grabbed his tie and hauled him close. This kiss was every bit as brief as the one he'd given her, but it packed a wallop.

"Satisfied?" she asked afterward.

He smiled slowly. "What do you think?"

Julia shook her head and expelled a sigh. "I think you'd better put on the apron."

A moment later, clad in the apron and holding a

large knife in his hand, Julia set him up in front of a cutting board with washed stalks of celery.

"We'll start with something very basic. Sliced-up vegetables with dip as an appetizer."

"You weren't kidding about basic."

"I want to gauge your skill with a knife before I turn you loose." She pointed to the celery. "Trim each stalk at the bottom and at the top just down from the leaves. Then cut them into three equal pieces."

He did as instructed. "That was easy enough and I still have all of my fingers."

Alec wiggled the digits on his left hand for her benefit.

"Okay, wise guy, think you can manage the carrots without any tutoring? They need to be peeled, too." She pursed her lips. "It's best to do it over the sink."

On that advice, she handed him a funky little tool and made a shaving motion. How hard could it be? he thought. Five minutes later, peels were everywhere, including still on parts of the carrots, and he had skinned up a knuckle. He glanced over at Julia, who was holding back a grin. His ego should have felt bruised. Instead, he was enjoying himself. Immensely. He could hear cartoons playing on the television in the other room. Every now and then, one of her kids would laugh.

Home.

"I'm out of my element," he told Julia truthfully.

"But you're doing okay." She regarded the gnarled stumps of carrots. "It just takes practice."

"You make it seem so easy," he said quietly. He glanced around the tiny kitchen. "And I'm not talking about peeling carrots, in case you're wondering. I envy you, Julia."

"You do?"

He nodded. "And what you've created here for you and your kids."

"Mom." Danielle stood in the doorway. "Colin put his fan in his hair and now it's stuck."

Julia speared him with a wry look. "And you said you envy me."

When she returned a moment later, he had arranged the sorry-looking assortment of veggies on a plate.

"How's Colin?"

She shrugged and slipped a pair of scissors back into a drawer. "He's due for a haircut anyway. And it's summer, so a buzz cut won't look out of place."

"Sorry."

She shrugged again, unfazed. "It's not the first thing to become stuck in his hair. Sadly, I doubt it will be the last." She eyed the tray and teased, "That almost looks good enough to eat."

"Yeah. Cooking is kind of fun."

"Whoa! Whoa! Don't get ahead of yourself," she warned on a laugh. "We haven't even begun to cook."

"So, what do you consider what we've been doing?" His voice dropped as he spoke, and he ran a fingertip down the length of her bare arm. "Foreplay?"

"Prep work." But she shivered.

"Same difference."

"Really?" There was a ghost of a smile playing on Julia's lips when she said, "It's been a while, but I seem to remember foreplay differently."

That brought him up short. Alec had the feeling he knew exactly how far back that memory stretched.

"Maybe we should compare notes," he said.

Their gazes locked. Julia moistened her lips. "I'd be lying if I didn't say that's a tempting offer."

"But?"

Children's laughter drifted into the kitchen from the other room. She offered a lopsided smile. "There's your answer."

Alec wanted to resent the intrusion. In the past, he would have. *Children have a place and it's anywhere I'm not.* That infamous gaffe had been rooted in truth. But with Julia, the intrusion of her children seemed… right. Nor did it do anything to curtail his interest. He wanted her all the more. Forbidden fruit? He had a feeling it was nothing quite as uncomplicated as that.

"We'd better get back to preparing dinner."

"Have you been scared off?" She said it lightly.

His reply was blunt. "Not by a long shot."

"Alec—"

"Dinner." He nodded toward the stove. He knew enough to recognize that it was electric rather than gas. A large pot was on one of the front burners, steaming rising from its open top. A smaller pan was on the adjacent burner. "So, what now?"

She smoothed the hair away from her face, back to being cool and collected. Her voice was instructional when she said, "You can put the pasta in the water and give the tomato sauce a stir."

"We're having spaghetti?"

"I figured it would be quick and easy."

He smiled. "But I see that you didn't trust me to bring the water to a boil on my own."

She shrugged. "I knew you could figure it out. You're bright."

"Thanks."

He was getting ready to put the pasta in when she said, "You have to salt the water first."

She was standing at his elbow, and he knew the heat he felt wasn't coming only from the pot. He found himself hoping for laughter to float from the living room. This silence was too potent.

"Here." She poured salt into the palm of his hand.

After he dropped it into the water, he added the noodles. Then, because it seemed right, he draped his arm around her shoulder. The gesture was casual, friendly. Perfect in the same way the daisies were, on a table set with everyday dishes for four. When Julia looked up at him, his heart began hammering at a ridiculous pace.

Her gaze slid to his hand. "You sure did a job on your knuckles. Let's go bandage them up. There's time before the noodles are ready."

He followed her down the hallway off the kitchen to a full bath. Across from it, he could see into two small bedrooms. Her kids' rooms, based on the furnishings, which meant hers was the one at the end of the hall. The door was ajar. He could just make out the bottom of the bed. A robe was tossed over the footboard. Nothing fancy. It wasn't lacy or sheer. Rather, pink terry cloth. He sucked in a breath all the same.

At her questioning gaze he said, "You're not going to put antiseptic on the scrape, are you?"

She rolled her eyes. "You're as bad as Colin."

Alec sat on the closed lid of the toilet seat while she rooted around in the medicine cabinet, pulling out antiseptic spray and a box of bandages. In short order, she had disinfected and bandaged his wound.

"That wasn't so bad, was it?" she asked.

"No. Not bad," he agreed.

The setting was less than romantic, as was the situation. Neither seemed to matter. At the moment, all that mattered to Alec was that they were alone, in tight quarters, and he wanted Julia in a way that defied both reason and restraint.

"But maybe you should kiss it," he added.

He had a hold of her hand and tugged ever so slightly. She could have resisted. Instead, after a fleeting glance at the door, she stepped closer, between the V of his legs, and bent down. Their breath mingled, but she stopped before their mouths could meet. She closed her eyes and sighed.

He figured that would be the end of it. That somehow they would both summon up enough self-control to return to the kitchen and resume meal preparation. Julia apparently had other ideas. She cupped his face in both of her hands and brought her mouth down on his. Forget prim girl next door. Forget patient professional. She was greedy, desperate. A bona fide seductress. When he felt her teeth nip his lower lip, he was grateful to be sitting. He would have fallen over otherwise. The kisses they'd shared up till this point had been tame in comparison. Not that Alec had any complaints. *Right back at you,* he thought, feeling greedy and desperate and—oh, yeah—seduced.

He had the presence of mind to put his foot out and kick the door closed, lest her kids wander down the hall and get an eyeful. Then, his mouth still fused to Julia's, he worked his way to standing. That changed the angle and gave him the advantage. He deepened the kiss. He might have been able to keep his hands on the relative safety of her waist had she not brought hers around to his chest. Her fingers fiddled with the placket of buttons on his shirt, but she didn't undo them. For the most part, the apron's bib was in the way. Still, she was testing her restraint. And his. To see who would buckle first?

She won.

On a groan, he pulled the soft cotton jersey from the waistband of her shorts and slipped his hands under her T-shirt. Her skin was warm and incredibly soft. He wanted access to more of it, all of it. He found the clasp of her bra and worked it free, then cupped her breasts in his hands. When his thumbs brushed over the nipples, Julia's ragged breathing turned into a moan. His control frayed even more. It might have snapped completely had a shriek not sounded from down the hall.

"Mom!" Danielle screamed. "The water is boiling over."

They sprung apart. Julia tugged down her blouse and tucked it back in, avoiding eye contact as she did so. Alec scrubbed a hand over his face, grateful to be wearing an apron. When she opened the door, her children were standing there, their eyes round with questions.

"What were you doing in there?" Colin asked.

"Your mom was just bandaging my knuckle. I scraped it up pretty good with the peeler."

Colin seemed to accept the explanation. "Did she put the spray on it?" He scrunched up his face. "That stuff really stings."

"She did."

"I hope you asked her to kiss it afterward."

"Uh, yeah. I did." He felt heat creep into his cheeks.

"That makes everything feel better," Colin said with an authoritative nod.

Not everything, Alec thought. His gaze turned to Danielle. She was older, wiser, shrewder. And, unless he missed his guess, she also was ticked off.

There was no time to contemplate that. The smoke alarm began to wail. All four of them rushed to the kitchen, where the pot containing the pasta was oozing a white froth over the edges and onto the burner. Julia grabbed a pair of potholders and pulled it away, waving frantically to clear the smoke. Colin ran out and returned a moment later with the miniature fans Alec had bought. He switched his on and handed the other one to Danielle. Then they pointed them in the direction of the smoking stovetop.

"I knew I bought those for a reason," Alec said.

Julia's laughter bubbled out, competing with the alarm. It was just this side of hysterical.

They wound up ordering a pizza, which they had delivered. Afterward, even though Julia told him he didn't need to stick around, he sat cross-legged with the kids on the floor and played a couple games of Trouble, which was appropriate, Alec decided, because, he was definitely feeling as if he'd gotten more than he'd bargained for.

Amazingly, Julia was sorry to see the evening end, even if parts of it had been awkward, others erotic, and all of it had left her questioning her sanity. She walked Alec to the door just after nine, surprised that he'd stayed so long. She'd certainly given him reasons to leave at the earliest opportunity. In addition to Colin's fan-in-the-hair high jinks and the near fire that had spoiled their bathroom interlude, Danielle had eyed him stonily all through their meal and then sulked the rest of the evening.

"Dinner didn't go quite how I planned," Julia admitted with a shake of her head. She forced her tone to remain light and focused on the meal. "But consider it a lesson for Saturday. Never leave a boiling pot unattended."

"Good advice." Alec jingled his car keys in his hand. His gaze was focused on her mouth. "I'd like to kiss you good-night, but I won't."

Something had to be said. She wouldn't bother pretending that the old boundaries needed to be restored. They'd pushed too far beyond those now to go back, even if she wanted to. That meant new ones had to be determined, discussed. Above all, sanity—hers—had to be restored. She glanced behind her and lowered her voice. "Um, about what happened in the bathroom—"

He cut off her words by laying a finger against her lips.

"Let's leave that for another time." He smiled, turned. She thought she heard him whistling as he bounded down the steps. Then he was gone and she was left to face the firing squad.

Sure enough, in the living room, Danielle was sitting on the couch, arms crossed, eyes narrowed, lips twisted in a scowl.

Uh-oh.

"What's wrong, honey?" Julia asked, even though she was sure she knew.

"Did you kiss him good-night?" her daughter demanded.

"No."

"But you wanted to."

From the time they could talk, Julia had drummed into her kids the importance of being forthright. So, as much as she would have liked to avoid the subject, she couldn't without being a hypocrite.

She replied honestly, "Yes, I did."

Her daughter's face crumpled. Danielle wasn't mad now. She looked lost, betrayed. Julia's *uh-oh* became *oh, no!*

"Well, I like him," Colin said, unaware of his sister's misery. "You can kiss him all you want, Mom."

"No, she can't!" Danielle cried before turning on her heel and fleeing to her room. A slamming door punctuated her departure.

Colin was immune to his sister's drama, but he scrunched up his face and asked, "If you kiss him, does that mean you're going to marry him?"

"No. It just means…" The problem was, Julia wasn't sure what it meant. Or even what she wanted it to mean. "It's getting late. Let's put the game away and get ready for bed."

TEN

—

    To Julia's relief, Alec's cooking stint at the family expo that weekend went off without a hitch. No knuckles got scraped. No pots boiled over. No smoke alarms were set off. In fact, from a public relations point of view, the segment exceeded her expectations.

Herman Geller had volunteered his five-year-old grandson, Sawyer, to act as Alec's co-chef. The two of them were charged with making reduced-sugar cinnamon bars, a good fit given Sawyer's high energy level. The tyke was rambunctious with a capital R and into everything, keeping Alec on his toes. More than one parent watching grimaced in sympathy when Sawyer knocked over a measuring cup full of sifted flour and then, as Alec stooped to clean up the mess, started adding eggs, shell and all, to the bowl.

Alec kept his composure and his sense of humor. While he came off as inept in the kitchen, he was endearingly so.

"I wouldn't mind having him come to my house,"

Julia overheard a woman standing behind her say to a friend.

To which the other woman replied, "Yeah, I'd be happy to give him a lesson or two in culinary basics."

Ribald laughter followed. Julia didn't know what possessed her, but she turned and said on a wink, "He's a quick study."

"Yeah? Lucky you." The first woman nudged her in the ribs with an elbow.

Lucky? Julia still wasn't sure. What she did know was that wise or not, she and Alec had crossed a line, and, even though she'd tried not to cross it in the beginning, they couldn't go back. Nor, now that she was being honest with herself, did she want to. That left her with one choice: Proceed with caution, with eyes wide open.

She wasn't worried about herself. She was a big girl and could handle the ramifications of whatever relationship grew up between her and Alec. But her kids were another matter.

Colin liked Alec. Of course, Colin liked *everyone*. He would welcome Alec into his life for as long as he stayed, happy to have someone to double-team with in Trouble and to regale with stories of his favorite action figures' adventures. But would he grow too attached?

And then there was Danielle. Based on her daughter's reaction Monday evening, there was no need to worry about her becoming overly fond of Alec. Julia had let her daughter sulk the remainder of that night, waiting till the following morning to speak to her. Danielle had made it plain that she didn't want her mother romantically involved with Alec. Period.

"We don't need him, Mom. He'll mess up *every-thing!*"

After that pronouncement, she'd stormed off again. She'd been giving Julia the silent treatment ever since. Even her usual begging to attend art camp had ceased.

One question remained to answer: What did Julia want?

Every time she recalled the chemistry between her and Alec, she told herself she knew. She wanted a little romance. Okay, sex, too. She was thirty-two years old, after all. And she hadn't had sex with a man since before Scott's death. Perhaps that was what this was all about. An itch that needed scratching.

But love and a long-term relationship? She wasn't sure she was ready for that. And she wasn't sure Alec was even capable of either. Companionship, adult conversation, a few sparks and a little fire? Oh, he could manage those. Especially the latter.

"You're quiet," he said to her now as his car idled at a stop light after they left the expo. "What's on your mind?"

Sparks, fire...sex. *Oh, boy.*

She flushed. "Nothing."

His brows rose. "So, I see."

Julia's parents had taken her kids for the weekend. That left her with a block of free time to fill as she saw fit. She had errands to run, laundry to tote down to the machines in the building's basement, an apartment in desperate need of cleaning. But whenever she looked at Alec, the only thing on her mind was picking up where they'd left off the other night before the smoke alarm sounded. Indeed, if there were a smoke alarm in his car, her thoughts would have set it off already.

She decided to change the subject. "I thought today went well. I heard a lot of positive comments while milling around in the crowd."

"Yeah." He grinned. He looked relaxed, one hundred and eighty degrees the opposite of the uptight, annoyed executive she'd first met in her office. "I actually had fun."

"That came through."

"Maybe the next time I cook for you, we won't have to order pizza."

The next time. He said those three little words with such ease that if Julia had been looking for strings and the possibility of commitment, she might have been tempted to believe they existed.

"Maybe," she allowed.

"What are you doing tonight?"

"For dinner?"

"Yeah. For dinner."

"I was just going to reheat some leftovers." She had to clear her throat before she could add, "Colin and Danielle are spending the night at my folks' house, so I'm on my own."

Even then, the words came out sounding hoarse.

He glanced over. His relaxed grin was gone. In its place was the beginnings of a smile that caused her blood to heat. If he couldn't read her mind, he was doing a good imitation of it.

"All by yourself, hmm?"

She nodded.

"Maybe we should do something about that."

He was leaving the ball in her court, giving her the option to toss it back, as well as a graceful way to drop it. She could say no, come up with an excuse. Even something as lame as the need to finish housework would suffice, since they both would know it wasn't the real reason she declined.

"Well?"

Saying no would be the smart thing. The responsible thing. The very thing she'd been doing for way too long. It was time for a change, the rebel inside of her whispered. She decided to listen to it and asked, "What do you have in mind?"

"A lot more than dinner, but we'll start with that." He winked and she swore she felt sparks shower her skin.

They made plans for seven o'clock. Julia left the choice of restaurant to him. She couldn't think clearly enough to pick one. She could barely think at all. As soon as she got home, she grabbed the cordless phone off the coffee table in the living room and dialed her sister's number in a panic.

"Help!" she shouted when Eloise came on the line.

"Julia? My God! What's wrong?"

"I have a date." She sank onto the couch.

"A date?" There was a smile in her sister's voice when she added, "That doesn't sound like an emergency as much as a reason to celebrate. Maybe even declare a national holiday."

"Eloise."

"Sorry. I'm guessing the problem is that the date is with your gorgeous client."

"How did you know?"

"Lucky guess," Eloise replied dryly. Then she asked, "Hey, don't you have a rule against that?"

"I did. I should." Julia pulled one of Colin's hard-plastic action figures from behind her and wilted back on the couch. "Maybe that's why I'm calling you. So you can talk me out of it."

"What's the real reason you want me to talk you out of it?" Eloise asked shrewdly.

"Well, for starters, I know this won't go anywhere. I'm attracted to him. *Really, really* attracted. But I think it might be a mistake to start something."

"Back up a step. Why are you so sure this won't go anywhere?"

"How long have you got?" Julia replied dryly.

"As long as it takes. That's what sisters are for."

And didn't Julia know it. Eloise had always been her sounding board and biggest cheerleader, but never more so than since Scott's death.

She took a deep breath and exhaled slowly. "First of all, I don't think Alec is looking for anything permanent." Except for a home, she thought, and felt an ache build in her chest. "He's got some...baggage," she told Eloise, and then filled in her sister on Alec's parents and his emotionally sterile upbringing.

"Poor guy. Just goes to show that money can't buy happiness," Eloise said. "But if you like him..."

"I do. But what about Danielle and Colin? I have to think about them, too."

"Don't they like him?"

Julia worried her lip. "It's a fifty-fifty split. Colin thinks Alec's fun. Danielle doesn't want him around at all and to drive home the point, she's not speaking to me."

Eloise didn't sound surprised by this news. "Danielle isn't going to like anyone you bring home, in part because she's old enough to remember Scott. Besides, she's a lot like you, Julia. Stubborn, picky and opinionated."

"I'm not—"

"You are," Eloise interrupted. "I love you anyway."

"El, I don't want Colin and Danielle to get too used to him being around. You know how kids are. They read too much into things."

"Just the kids?" When Julia said nothing, Eloise went on. "So, if you're so sure this thing with Alec won't amount to anything, I don't see the problem. Go out on a date tonight. Dress up and look gorgeous. Enjoy yourself. The kids are at Mom and Dad's. You don't have to worry about a curfew or paying a sitter. You've earned a night out."

"I have." She nodded vigorously, even though her sister couldn't see her. "I'm being stupid, aren't I?"

"An absolute idiot."

Julia continued, working to convince herself more than her sister. "It's dinner out at a restaurant. One date. I've done that a few times in the past few years. And it's not like Alec and I haven't spent time together already, so there won't be any awkward silences or anything."

"Right."

"So, you don't think I'm making a mistake by going out with him?"

"No. But I think you need to be honest with yourself. It's not just a date. As you said, you've had a few of those since Scott died. You're in a panic because you like Alec. A lot. And it scares you. A lot. We wouldn't be having this conversation otherwise."

"I do. And it does."

"Take it one day and one date at a time."

Julia swallowed and gave voice to one of her many fears where Alec was concerned. It wasn't the biggest one, but it was on her mind. "El, I haven't had sex with a man in a really long time."

"Well, I can assure you, it hasn't changed," her sister replied dryly. "Are you thinking about...you know... tonight?"

"No! Yes. No!" She covered her eyes with her free hand, then parted her fingers as she added, "Maybe, but probably not."

"As long as you're sure."

"I'm not planning it. But when I'm with Alec, things tend to...happen." Another of her fears bubbled to the surface then. "You don't think he'll expect it, do you? I mean, on a first date. Even though this isn't really a first date. But it sort of is."

"Are *you* expecting it?"

"Not expecting it any more than I'm planning it, but I've been *thinking* about it. It's hard not to think about it when I'm around him." Even talking about him had her temperature threatening to rise.

"My advice is to be prepared, then, if you know what I mean."

Julia swallowed. Hearing it put like that made her feel like a teenager, even if her sister's suggestion made perfect sense. A strangled laugh slipped out.

"I feel like an idiot. I'm thirty-two years old."

"As you said, it's been a long time." Eloise's tone turned sober then. "I know how serious you take your responsibilities as a parent, especially since Scott died. You've put your kids first in all things."

Julia straightened to a sitting position on the couch, her gaze on the action figure that was now lying on the coffee table. "They're my top priority."

"I'm not saying they shouldn't be. But you've neglected yourself, your needs, and that's not healthy, Jul. I'm glad to see you interested enough in a man to be, well, acting like an idiot."

"Thanks. I think."

"Have fun tonight." Eloise waited a beat before adding, "Wear something so sexy that he'll want to skip dinner."

Alec's mouth went dry when Julia opened the door. He'd seen her in professional attire and outfitted in casual clothes. He'd never seen her in a dress such as this one, with a neckline that scooped low to offer a tantalizing view of cleavage and a pair of strappy high heels that made her legs appear a good foot longer.

His breath came out on a ragged groan. He reached up to loosen his tie before he realized he wasn't wearing one. He'd gone with a dress shirt and lightweight gabardine trousers.

"You look amazing."

Her smile was a beguiling mixture of shyness and victory. "Thank you. I hope it's not too much. I don't get a chance to dress up very often."

"Then we'll do this right," he decided. He'd made

reservations at a much-hyped new French restaurant on Michigan Avenue that had opened earlier in the month. He wanted to give her a night out to remember. But now, it wouldn't do. He pulled out his cell phone, sending her a wink as he dialed. "Georgio, it's Alec McAvoy...good, good. And you...? Hey, I need a favor... yes, I know it's last-minute and you're probably booked solid, but... Yeah...? Eight o'clock sounds perfect."

He disconnected and smiled smugly.

"Who was that?"

"The maître d' at Fazzello's."

Her eyes widened. "You got us a table? But that place is impossible to get into, let alone at the last minute." Reservations were taken months in advance.

"I know the owner. We attended the same boarding school." They'd both been weekenders, as the staff called students who stayed on when class wasn't in session. As such they'd stuck together. Alec reached out and ran his knuckles lightly down Julia's cheek. "It looks like we have some time to kill."

They were still standing in her doorway. He watched her swallow before she took a step back. "Then I guess you should come in."

Her apartment was quiet without the kids. And free of interruptions, a fact they both were achingly aware of, if the way she was biting her lower lip was any indication.

"Do you want some wine? I have a bottle of red I could open."

He shook his head. Took a step closer.

"Iced tea? I made a pitcher earlier today."

"No thanks." Another step.

She put a hand on her chest, blew out a breath. "I think we need to, um, talk about...about things."

He was near enough now to touch her, so he did, fingering one of the thin straps of her dress. His heart was starting to hammer. Go slow, he reminded himself. He kissed her cheek, the spot just in front of her ear and then started down her neck.

"What things?" he asked when he reached her shoulder.

"I haven't got a clue." And then she cupped his face and kissed him back.

ELEVEN

———

June gave way to July, and July to August. Alec dropped heavily into a chair in his apartment's living room. It was late on a Sunday night one week into the month and he'd only just gotten in. He'd spent the weekend in New York, where he'd taped a segment for a nationally televised morning program and spent all day Saturday at a huge toy store that was raising money and awareness for childhood diseases.

He'd gone alone, although Julia had called, texted and emailed him several times over the past couple of days. It wasn't the same, though. He'd wanted her with him.

He scrubbed a hand down his face in frustration, not so much amazed at how quickly she'd gotten under his skin, but how one-sided it all seemed to be. For the first time in his life, Alec was with a woman he actually wanted to draw closer, a woman who knew more about him and his dysfunctional family than any other ever had...and still liked him. A woman who wasn't interested in his bank account or intrigued by the celebrities his parents knew. She liked him. She'd said as much. But she'd also established boundaries between them, an emotional cutoff point against which he was already butting.

He and Julia hadn't spoken about her boundaries. They didn't appear to be up for negotiation, although Alec knew she had adjusted them once already when the two of them became intimately involved. The old Alec would have accepted them. Hell, he would have been happy to have them. He wasn't that Alec any longer. Looking back, he could see that he'd started changing the day he'd met her. Not his image, but his outlook. He was a better man now, of that he was certain. But was he good enough for Julia and her children? The question nagged at him.

The phone rang. He knew it was Julia even before he saw her name on the caller ID display.

"Isn't this past your bedtime?" he teased in lieu of a greeting.

He pictured her wearing modest cotton and tucked into the very bed in which they'd made love the first time. A bed he had yet to return to. He hadn't breached even the front door of her apartment since that evening. Julia came to him, when time permitted and the opportunity presented itself. Other than stolen kisses and hasty couplings wedged into their busy daytime schedules, they didn't see one another. Each weekday evening, she went home to her children. Alec returned to his apartment—alone and increasingly edgy and uneasy.

"It is past my bedtime," she admitted on a low chuckle. "But I wanted to say good-night."

"I wish you were here to do it in person."

It was a futile wish, he knew, so it surprised him when she said, "How about you hold that thought for Wednesday?"

"What's Wednesday?"

"Well, Danielle leaves for art camp on Monday." Julia had finally, after much emotional hand-wringing, agreed to let her daughter go. Alec had played a role in convincing her. It was different, he'd assured her, for a child to go away when they knew they would return shortly and to a home where they would be both missed and welcomed back. She was saying, "And because Colin is feeling very left out, my parents are having him come to stay with them Wednesday through the weekend. So, I'll be on my own."

Alec should have been pleased. They could be together, alone and uninterrupted, for four nights. *Only* four nights. For reasons he didn't care to dwell on, he felt irritated. Make the most of it, he reminded himself and forced a smile into his voice. "How about coming over Wednesday evening then? I can try my hand at cooking again and, if the weather is nice, we can eat out on the roof."

"I like that idea."

"You can stay the night if you want. Pack a bag and you can leave for work from here in the morning." It was an offer he didn't often make. It seemed natural with Julia.

Still, he wasn't surprised when she declined. "Thanks, but I'll go home."

Boundaries, he thought again, feeling hemmed in. They talked about work after that, a safe subject that he suspected she chose for just that reason. She gave him an update of his week's itinerary. He had a return spot on the first blog Julia had set up. Now that the One Big Family campaign was winding down, Julia had him hitting as many of the places he'd visited in the beginning as possible. He wouldn't go so far as to say that his image was fully repaired, but it had recovered substantially. Julia was due the credit for that. Alec had fought her in the beginning, out of pride and pique more than anything else, but she knew what she was doing.

Best For Baby's stock had rebounded by several points in the past month alone. These days, when the company made headlines, it was because of the new line of organic toddler food it had unveiled rather than its bachelor CEO's unfortunate case of foot-in-mouth disease.

The board of directors was pleased, so much so that Alec no longer felt as if his professional neck were waiting under the sharp blade of an executioner's ax. Now, however, he felt as if something else was hanging over his head, a sense of impending doom that he preferred not to think about.

Their conversation wound down. He heard Julia yawn. Her kids would be asleep, tucked into their beds just down the hall from her room. Safe. Loved. Secure in their home. He glanced around his tidy apartment. It was so quiet and empty in a way that had nothing to do with its Spartan décor.

"It's late," he said. "I'll let you go."

They said goodbye and he hung up, left with the

unshakable feeling that he didn't have enough of a hold on her to let her go.

"So, big plans with Alec this week since you'll be kidless for four entire nights?" Eloise asked.

Her sister had stopped by Julia's office after an appointment in the city. The two of them were at a restaurant enjoying a glass of iced tea on the cordoned-off patio as they waited for their salads to arrive.

"We're having dinner on Wednesday. He's going to cook for me."

"I bet." Eloise waggled her eyebrows. "Are you staying over at his place?"

"No. I don't think that's a good idea."

"Hmm." Eloise sipped her tea.

"What *hmm?*"

"Nothing. I just thought you would since you didn't have to hurry home. But I guess it's not surprising that he didn't suggest it. Single men tend to see overnight stays in their domain as tantamount to a commitment. They like the option of being the one to leave first, and you can't do that when it's your own place."

"Actually, he did suggest it." An ache formed in the back of her throat. She soothed it with a sip of tea.

"But you'd rather go home?"

"I'm trying very hard to keep things between Alec and me…simple. I think that is the best solution in the long run."

Eloise frowned. "Why? I know you felt that way in the beginning. You wanted a little romance and adult time, and weren't looking for strings, but, Jul." Eloise grabbed Julia's hand and squeezed to give her words emphasis. "Whenever his name is brought up in conversation you all but glow. Mom and Dad have noticed it, too. And I've got to tell you, they're wondering why you haven't brought him by for dinner."

Her stomach knotted. It had been doing that a lot lately where Alec was concerned. "You know why."

"Danielle will come around," Eloise assured her. "For that matter, how can you expect her to soften toward Alec if she never has any interaction with him?"

It was a logical question, except that it assumed the relationship with Alec would be long-lasting. On her own, Julia might have been willing to risk placing a bet. If she lost, her heart would be the only casualty.

"Alec and I are enjoying one another as well as our time together. That's all I want at this point."

But Eloise was shaking her head. "It's not all you want. It's all you think you have a *right* to want. Do you love him?"

"No!" But that ache was back in her throat and she knew that no amount of cold tea would soothe it. "It wouldn't be a good idea to fall in love with Alec."

"So, he's not the warm-and-fuzzy, good-with-kids executive you've helped convince Best For Baby consumers that he is?"

"You're playing devil's advocate," Julia accused.

Eloise merely shrugged. "And you're changing the subject."

Touché, she thought, and answered the question.

"When he's around children at the events I've booked, he does well enough. He's still a little stiff at times, but kids respond to him." Julia smiled and, with a shake of her head, added, "And so do their mothers."

"But you have reservations about having him in your life."

"He's in my life," Julia shot back.

Eloise wasn't buying it. "No. You've allowed him into a *portion* of your life. The part where you are a single woman. We both know what a small slice of yourself you're allowing him."

Julia didn't care for the guilt nipping at her. "He hasn't complained."

"And if he does?"

Would he? Did she want him to? She couldn't answer her own questions, so she answered Eloise's. "When and if that happens, I'll deal with it."

How exactly was a mystery.

Since she would be driving home later that evening anyway, Julia declined Alec's offer to come pick her up on Wednesday. She knocked off work just after four, in part because she knew Alec would be at his office until at least five o'clock. These days, he no longer stayed past six, and he hadn't clocked in on a weekend since their first date.

After going home to change clothes, she stopped at a market to select some produce. Alec said he would cook for her, but she planned to bring the fixings for a salad. Not much could go wrong with fresh greens.

"Hey, Hank!" she called to the guard as she crossed the lobby to the elevator just after six.

"Hi, Julia. If you're here to see Mr. McAvoy, he's not here yet."

"Oh." She shifted the bag of groceries to her other arm and glanced toward the pair of leather chairs that were angled together in front of the floor-to-ceiling window. "I'll wait over here."

She was leafing through an old copy of a news magazine when a woman tottered in on a pair of four-inch-high stilettos. Julia placed the woman in her late fifties, even though she was trying to look like someone in her late twenties. Her hair was long and bleached platinum-blond. Her skin was a couple of shades too tanned to look natural and it was pulled suspiciously taut over a pair of painfully prominent cheekbones. Her plumped-up lips were slicked in the shimmery pink gloss girls not much older than Danielle favored. Her trim, hourglass figure was enviable, but it still looked out of place tucked into a miniskirt and off-the-shoulder, peasant-style blouse. Every reality television show seemed to have one or more women on it who looked just like this one. The miniature dog she held in her arms merely finished off the cliché.

Something about the woman was familiar. Julia knew what it was as soon as she heard her ask Hank, "I'm here to see Alec McAvoy. I've been trying to reach him at his office, but he hasn't returned my call. I'm desperate to speak with him. Is he in?"

Good God! It was Alec's mother. Term loosely applied. Julia felt bile rise in her throat along with a good amount of anger. Did that woman know what she'd done? Had she any clue how much she had hurt and harmed Alec with her careless disregard? Looking at her now, it was hard to believe she had any remorse.

Hank glanced Julia's way, but she pretended to read the magazine as emotions churned.

"Mr. McAvoy hasn't arrived yet. I'm not sure when

to expect him. I could take a message if you can't wait," he offered.

"Oh, that's all right." Over the top of the magazine, Julia saw the woman sidle closer to Hank and flash a blindingly white smile. "Maybe you could let me into his apartment to wait. I know I don't look old enough, but I swear I'm his mother."

Hank scratched the back of his head just below his security cap. "Sorry, but I'm not allowed to do that, ma'am."

She shrugged. "Well, then, I guess I'll just have to sit over there."

She took the chair opposite Julia's. The little dog yipped twice before growling.

"Oh, look. Valentino likes you," Brooke McAvoy said.

Julia worked up a smile. Oh, but this was awkward. Should she introduce herself and save Alec from having to do so when he arrived? It would mean having to make polite conversation in the interim, but she decided to do it. She cleared her throat.

"I couldn't help but overhear you say that you're Alec's mother."

"That's right. Brooke McAvoy." She studied Julia with critical eyes. "And you are...a friend of my son's?"

Even though the moniker didn't quite fit, Julia nodded. "That's right. I'm Julia Stillwell."

She considered offering a hand in greeting, just to be polite, but the little dog was still growling low in its throat, and Julia was afraid it might bite her.

"Do you live in the building?" Brooke asked.

"Actually, like you, I'm here waiting for Alec. We're having dinner."

Brooke's gaze moved to the grocery bag, took a detour to Julia's A-line cotton skirt and casual wedge sandals and then returned to her face. She'd been sized up and, unless she missed her guess, found lacking.

"Have you known my son very long?"

"A couple of months."

"Really?" Brooke wrinkled her nose and her tone turned sympathetic. "I'm afraid he hasn't mentioned you."

Under other circumstances, such a remark might sting. Coming as it did from a woman who suffered chronic maternal apathy, it merely aroused pity. Alec had told Julia enough about his mother that she knew he didn't confide in her.

The doors to the lobby swung open then and Alec rushed in, saving her from the chore of formulating a reply. He was wearing his usual suit-and-tie attire, and carrying a laptop in a bag that hung from his shoulder. He looked every inch the high-powered professional he was, yet he took time on this day to smile and call out a friendly greeting to Hank, something Julia doubted Alec would have done not so long ago. He'd changed so much. It occurred to her then that she had as well. Five paces from the elevator, he spied Julia and then his gaze slid to his mom. His smile evaporated. He sucked in a breath and expelled it as he crossed the lobby to where they sat. Both women rose.

"Mother." He kissed Brooke's cheek, but only because she tilted her head toward him in anticipation. The dog yapped as he did so and grabbed a mouthful of Alec's tie. As he fought to free it, he said, "I thought when we spoke earlier today that I made it clear I had plans for tonight."

"You did, and I'm not here to spoil them. But I called back several times and you were unavailable. I wanted to see if you had...reconsidered." She glanced toward Julia before finishing.

A muscle worked in his jaw. He was angry, that much was clear. She doubted he knew that he also looked sad and sick at heart.

"Julia, would you excuse us for a moment?" He handed her his key ring. "Why don't you go on up? I shouldn't be long."

"All right." Julia smiled at Brooke. Although it had been anything but, she told her, "It was nice to meet you, Mrs. McAvoy."

Twenty minutes passed before she heard the door open. A thud sounded—the laptop being deposited on the table in the foyer?—and then heavy footsteps on the wood floor. Julia was in Alec's kitchen. She hadn't spent much time in it, but she knew her way around well enough to find a pair of wineglasses and pour them both a glass of merlot. She met him in the living room, where he stood in front of the large glass window with his back ramrod-straight and his head bowed.

"Here."

He took the glass she held out. "Thanks."

"Everything okay?" she inquired.

He looked weary and resigned, but he nodded and took a sip. Then he set his glass aside, reached for hers and did the same. Finally, he wrapped his arms around her. They stood embracing for several minutes, neither saying a word.

When he finally drew back, Julia asked, "Do you want to talk about it?"

He blew out a sigh. "Do you really want to hear this?"

She nodded, then she swallowed as it occurred to her this was another kind of intimacy, the sort upon which real relationships were formed. Lovers didn't share confidences. Couples did.

"It's the same old story. She and my father need money." His laugher was harsh, bitter. "They have an active social life, you know. Parties to attend and parties to host. And only the best vintages of wine and choices cuts of meat will do."

"The trust fund," Julia said, recalling what he'd told her about his late grandfather's estate.

Alec nodded. "They've already blown through this month's funds. Of course, this happens pretty much every month." He added wryly, "They have champagne-and-caviar taste on a champagne-only budget."

Which meant Alec was cast in the unenviable role of being a parent to his parents. He appeared to know what she was thinking.

"'Sometimes I think my grandfather arranged his will this way so that my parents and I would be forced to have a relationship." Alec shook his head. "Not that you can really call what we have a relationship."

"I'm sorry, Alec."

Relationships were about give and take. They were about sharing more than a name or proximity. They required trust and an abiding commitment. Julia felt an unmistakable stab of guilt.

"Not much of a pedigree, is it?" Alec reached for his wine again. Before taking a sip, he added, "It's a good thing no reporters managed to dig up too much of my background and spread it around. Even someone as skilled in remaking images as you are wouldn't have been able to save my job then."

"You're not your parents, Alec."

"No, but they made me. We're shaped by the people around us." He nodded in her direction. "You believe that."

An alarm bell sounded in her head, but she said, "I don't know what you mean."

"You don't let just anyone around your children. You take care to protect them from bad influences and poor examples."

She swallowed. It wasn't only guilt she felt now, but something suspiciously like shame that he might think she regarded him as a bad influence or poor example.

"I love my kids," she said slowly.

"I know that you do. They're lucky. Lucky to be loved and wanted. Lucky to have someone like you who places their welfare first." He turned back to the window and finished off his wine. His back was no longer ramrod-straight. His shoulders were bowed, as if they carried the weight of the world. "I guess I'd started to hope..."

"Alec?"

He turned and all traces of vulnerability were gone, replaced with a manufactured smile. "Let's talk about something else. I bought a couple of thick steaks for tonight." And a gas barbecue grill, too. It's a stainless steel beast that took two delivery men to haul in."

Because Julia didn't know what else to say, she let him change the subject. "I didn't realize you knew how to grill."

"I don't. Well, not exactly." He lifted his shoulders. "I watched a video on YouTube. How hard can it be?"

The steaks he made were the texture of shoe leather and they tasted about the same. Grilling wasn't as easy as the salesman in the home improvement store made it sound or the guy in the internet video made it look, Alec decided as he cleared the table a couple hours later. Julia helped him.

She'd been quiet through most of their meal. What conversation they had amounted to small talk. Probably meeting his mother had scared her, giving her the glimpse it had of the woman who'd helped mold him and his value system. After all, Brooke tried to look like a teenager only to succeed in acting like a child: egocentric and spoiled.

"I heard from Danielle," Julia said out of the blue.

"She arrived safe and sound at camp, I assume."

"She did. She sounded so excited and happy. I'm glad I agreed to let her go."

"And Colin? Have you heard from him as well?" Alec didn't really need to ask. He knew she would have, calling him first if need be.

Sure enough, she said, "I phoned my parents right before I came here. Colin said his cousins were coming over in the morning to spend the whole day." She rinsed their plates and stacked them on the counter next to the sink. Her brow furrowed when she added, "He said to tell you that he and his grandfather would be making cookies tomorrow. He said you would know why he was so happy about that."

Alec grinned and at her questioning glance, shrugged. "It's a secret."

"Oh." She dried her hands on the dish towel.

She looked so pretty, standing in his kitchen. So... right. And the kitchen, hell, his entire apartment, had warmed by several degrees and become more welcoming with her in it. Almost like a home. He pushed away the longing, the same way that, earlier, he had quashed his vulnerability.

Still, he heard a damning trace of wistfulness in his tone when he told her, "My real estate agent called just before I left the office today. He claims to have found exactly what I'm looking for."

In the past couple of months, Julia had accompanied Alec when he'd looked at two other listings. Both had been large and impressive and, because of the current market, priced right. As investments, they would have been hard to beat. But neither had made him feel settled or compelled to offer a down payment, much less to put down roots.

"Have you set a time to go see it?"

"Not yet." Alec had waited to get her schedule. Now he asked, "Do you still want to come with me?"

"Why wouldn't I?" Her tone held a subtle challenge that made him want to smile in relief.

"Tomorrow then? After work?"

"I'll meet you at your office and we can drive together from there," she suggested.

* * *

When Julia woke in the morning, she stretched out a
hand on her bed. She didn't realize what she was reaching for until her hand came up empty. She'd sought
Alec. But, of course, she was alone. Her choice. Even
her children were gone, making the apartment un-
naturally quiet.

The previous night, at his apartment, she and Alec
had made love in his bed before she'd roused herself,
dressed and left just before midnight. As many times
as she told herself it made sense—this careful way she
had compartmentalized her life, keeping the man she
was dating from the children she adored—she was beginning to realize they couldn't go on this way.

She'd seen it in his gaze last night when she was
leaving him. Even before that, she'd heard it in his
voice when he'd told her about his parents. Their relationship was hobbled. As such, it could only extend
so far before it foundered and fell apart. Were they already at that point?

In the dim early morning light, her gaze drifted to
her left hand, the fingers of which were curled into
the covers on the empty side of the bed. During her
marriage, Julia had slept in that spot, switching sides
after Scott's death and then only because she'd sworn
that at times she could still smell his scent on the mat-
tress. It had been a long time since she'd turned her
head into the sheets and inhaled deeply, searching for
comfort. Now, she relaxed her hand. This morning
marked the first time she'd found herself reaching
for someone else.

Surrounded by the lonely quiet of the morning, Julia accepted a truth she hadn't wanted to see coming. She'd fallen in love again.

TWELVE

———

The house where Alec and Julia were to meet Fred was in the same neighborhood as the first one they'd seen together. This house, however, was several hundred square feet smaller and vaguely cottage-esque thanks to its cobblestone and cedar-shake-siding façade.

Alec pulled the car to the curb, leaving the engine and air-conditioning running while they waited for his agent to arrive.

From the passenger seat, Julia said, "I like the exterior. And the landscaping is nice without being too ornate."

It did look welcoming with its curved walkway that was lined with cheery flowers. He didn't know enough about plants to know what they were called, but they were pink and white with waxy leaves, and apparently didn't mind the yard's abundance of shade.

Fred arrived. He parked in the driveway, his grin wide and just this side of smug as they walked with him to the front porch.

"Didn't I tell you it was perfect?"

"We haven't seen the inside yet," Alec reminded him.

Fred was undeterred. "Then let's not waste any more time out here."

He unlocked the front door and ushered them inside, offering a printout that detailed the home's key features. The foyer opened into a great room. The formal dining room in this house didn't come across as formal. No crystals dangled from its charming chandelier. Alec noticed that the electrical outlets were covered in plastic safety devices. This was a home where children lived and played, a suspicion confirmed a moment later when he spied a stickman-like drawing in red crayon on the wall in the kitchen.

Beside him, he heard Julia sigh.

"I love the floor plan. No matter where you are, you feel connected to the main living spaces." She nodded to French doors that led out to a patio. "I could stand here at the island, making dinner, and see the kids playing in the yard. And, oh, look, there's a swing set."

"The yard has a nice privacy fence," Fred pointed out. "Even without it, the lots here are generous enough that you wouldn't feel like you were right on top of your neighbors."

"I see what you mean." She tapped her lower lip in consideration. "There's plenty of room out there for a pool. I wouldn't want one now. I'd worry too much. But in another year or two, when they're older..."

She smiled absently, as if picturing it. Oh, yeah, she could see herself there, he decided. And no wonder.

Alec could see her there as well. With her children. The four of them together under the neatly pitched roof.

He'd never had one, but he knew it instantly. This was a home.

Excitement built, accompanied by rawboned fear. Maybe that was to be expected. Surely, a man walking the high wire without a net for the first time could be excused for the butterflies in his stomach. Julia glanced over and smiled at him. A look passed between them. She knew he felt the pull of the house, too. He smiled back.

The twenty minutes they spent on the rest of the walk-through was merely a formality. In his head, in his heart, the house was his. Next, he would set to work on making Julia and her children his as well.

"Oh, Alec, I'm so happy for you," Julia told him as they returned to the car. "Everything about that place is perfect."

His agent was going to write up an offer as soon as he got back to his office. Alec wasn't interested in haggling. He'd told Fred to make it for the full amount of asking. Hell, he would give them more if need be. He wanted this house and the bit of heaven he'd glimpsed standing inside of it with Julia.

"It's something all right." He grinned and gave the steering wheel a celebratory thump with the heels of his hands. "A real home."

His gaze connected with Julia's. Emotions tumbled inside of him, their once-sharp edges worn smooth by the force. The words that went along with those emotions took form and begged for release, but they were so alien and new, and he felt so vulnerable, he swallowed them back.

"Let's celebrate," she said quietly. "At my place. You can stay overnight, if you'd like. I'll drive into work with you in the morning to pick up my car."

An entire night. It was a concession, a large one on her part, yet suddenly it wasn't enough. Not now that he'd found his home. Pieces tumbled into place. They'd been there all along, Alec realized. He just hadn't understood how they fit together.

He did now.

He cleared his throat. "We're not far from your parents' house. Why don't we stop in and see Colin before heading back to the city?"

The suggestion was met with a gut-hallowing amount of silence. Finally, she said, "I'd rather we didn't. He's having fun, but if he sees me, he'll probably want to come home."

What she meant was that she still wasn't willing to mix the two halves of her life.

Alec nodded and managed to keep his expression neutral, even as that sharp blade he'd feared looming over his neck slipped from its perch. The pain was sharp, and the blow, he knew, fatal. Even so, he debated his options as they drove back to the city.

He could continue to pretend that all was well. That everything between them was perfect and satisfying. Their affair might last a few weeks longer. Their time spent together would be bittersweet as each of them let go. Or maybe it would just be bitter. He'd never been in love before.

The other option was to call Julia on the fabrication

she'd just fed him regarding Colin. Funny, how such a lie wouldn't have mattered overmuch to Alec in the past. But then he'd never before been emotionally invested in a relationship with actual ties to sever once things had run their inevitable course. Letting go was easy when you'd never been holding on.

Tell her you love her, a voice inside his head insisted. The problem was, Alec could see things too clearly from Julia's point of view. He meant what he'd said to her the other night about his pedigree. The truth was, he was a bad investment, hardly the sort of man a smart single woman wanted around as she raised her children. Even if that man realized he loved those children as much as he loved their mother and wanted them in his life.

He'd found a home at last, but that didn't mean he truly understood the dynamics of one. He suspected he had much to learn, and as patient a teacher as Julia could be, who could blame her for not wanting to let him try out his new skills on her kids?

When they reached her apartment forty minutes later, Alec had reached a decision. He bypassed a parking spot and stopped in the loading zone adjacent to the building's front entrance, where he shifted the car into Park, but didn't kill the engine.

"You're not coming in, are you?" she said quietly.

"No. I'll have your car brought over first thing in the morning." Concentrating on those small details helped.

She nodded. "We're not just talking about tonight, are we?"

Anger born of pain flashed and had him pointing

out, "I won't be welcome in your home another time anyway, not unless your children aren't there, which, let's face it, is a rare occurrence."

"They're my children!"

He reined in his emotions. Reason was called for here. "I know. I admire the way you are with them, how much you love them. You're the kind of mother all children should have, and I wouldn't want you to treat your kids any other way, especially on account of me." Anger left, replaced by sadness. "But you lead two separate lives, Julia, and I'm only part of one."

She didn't deny it. Rather, she said, "I thought it would be best that way."

He didn't want to ask, but the part of him that felt as if it were dying needed to know. "And now? Is it still best?"

He counted the beats of his busted heart in the silence that followed. Fourteen in all, each one more painful than the last.

"Yes. I'm sorry." As she studied the hands clenched in her lap, a tear slipped down her cheek. "I didn't mean to hurt you."

Because he was hurt, he blurted out, "And I didn't mean to fall in love with you."

Her head snapped up at that. Her expression was panicked. He'd been hoping to see pleasure. "Alec—" she began.

He shook his head. "My problem. Not yours."

"I didn't think things would end this way," she said sadly.

Unspoken was that she had expected things to end.

He couldn't fault her for that. Hadn't he thought so too in the beginning?

Julia leaned over the console and pressed a kiss to his cheek before getting out of the car. He waited until she was inside the building to start the Porsche's engine and drive away.

THIRTEEN

—

The beginning of the school year was always hectic as Julia and her children settled back into a routine. But by the end of October, everything still seemed off. Julia blamed it on the fact that she was so busy at work. She wanted it that way. Busy meant she wouldn't have time to think about Alec.

Or the fact that he loved her.

Or that she loved him, too.

She'd taken on three new clients, including a high-profile fitness guru who'd been photographed smoking cigarettes and eating fast food on several occasions. It didn't help that the woman was unrepentant. Her do-as-I-say-not-as-I-do attitude had cost her several public appearances and a couple of sponsorship opportunities. She made resurrecting Alec's image seem like a walk in the park.

Julia's efforts on behalf of Best For Baby had wound down, so much so that she had appointed Sandy to handle most of the contact with Alec. Avoiding him completely, however, was impossible. When they did see one another, their conversations were utilitarian or painfully polite.

So, she knew from updating the address in his file that he'd moved into the bungalow on Cloverleaf Lane. She'd sent him a potted plant as a housewarming gift, signing the card on behalf of Stillwell Consulting. She'd received a thank-you in the mail last week. It was impersonal, too, and signed simply Alec. Still, she'd studied the card for several minutes, wondering if the stray pen stroke just above his name might indicate that he'd considered adding a closing remark. *Sincerely*, perhaps? Or *Love*? The possibility had caused her to cry.

Julia had been crying a lot since their breakup, though she did her best to hide it from her kids. They'd picked up on the fact that something was amiss, though. Just the previous night, Danielle had curled up on the couch with her while she'd sat with Colin watching one of his action hero movies.

"Do you miss Daddy?" she'd asked out of the blue.

"Of course I do."

"Is that why you're so sad lately?"

Colin stopped watching his show and both children had looked at her. "I'm not sad. I've just been busy."

"I think you need to get married again," Colin had announced.

Instead of immediately shooting down the idea, as Danielle had in the past, she had studied her mother and asked, "Would that make you happy, Mom?"

"I'm happy now." Julia had forced a smile.

Danielle's expression was full of skepticism. She wasn't the only one not buying it.

* * *

"Are you sure I look mean enough?" Colin asked. He was dressed as a pirate for Halloween, complete with an eye patch and a gray plastic hook over his hand. Julia had just finished drawing a scar on his cheek with her makeup.

"You look fierce," she assured him and plopped a triangular black cap on his head.

"Come on, Mom. We need to go. All the good candy will be gone if we don't start early," Danielle said from the doorway of the bathroom. She was a princess for the occasion, wearing a gemstone-studded tiara and a couple of yards of filmy pink tulle.

The plan was to drive to Julia's parents' house so that the kids could trick-or-treat in a neighborhood.

"Remember, we need to make a stop first."

Since she would be out that way, she'd sent Alec an email and told him she would be dropping off some feedback from a focus group she'd commissioned early in the summer. She could have sent the letters over by messenger. Or had them scanned in and sent electronically for that matter. But the plain truth was she wanted to see him in person, away from work. And having her kids with her was a way to let him know... well, she wasn't sure what it was supposed to let him know. Maybe it was her attempt at another apology.

A few minutes later, they were loaded in the car and started off.

"Do you wish you were a kid again when it's Halloween?" Colin asked from the backseat. "Adults miss all the fun."

"It's fun to hand out candy, too," she said.

Julia's thoughts turned to Alec. Would he be at the door in his new house, handing out goodies to the neighborhood children? When she reached his street, she drove slowly. Though it wasn't quite dark out, kids in costume were everywhere, followed by parents wearing coats to ward off the evening's chill. Porch lights were on up and down the block. Houses were lit up like the carved pumpkins resting near their front steps. The porch light was on at Alec's house, too. A jack-o'-lantern sat on the top step, candlelight flickering from behind a pair of asymmetrically carved eyes.

Alec opened the door even before she and the kids had climbed the steps. If she'd picked his clothes, this would have been the outfit she chose. Jeans and a rust-colored long-sleeved shirt, which he'd left untucked. Just the right amount of casual without being sloppy. He looked...gorgeous. And though she thought she was prepared to see him face-to-face, her knees wobbled a bit and the bruised edges of her heart began to ache.

"Hello, Julia," he said. His smile encompassed her children as well. "And you brought a princess and a pirate with you, I see."

Colin grinned and pulled up his eye patch. "It's me, Alec!" Then, not one to miss an opportunity, he stuck out his bag. "Trick or treat!"

Alec grabbed a handful of candy from the dish next to the door and dropped it inside. "What about you?" he said to Danielle.

She considered a moment before holding her bag out as well.

Just then, from behind Alec, came a howl and the

scramble of four feet seeking purchase on polished hardwood.

"Cool! A dog!" Colin shouted.

"It's a puppy," Danielle corrected. But her smile went all liquid at the sight of the golden retriever. It looked to be about three months old. Its paws belonged to a dog a dozen months older than that.

"You got a dog?" Julia said.

"Last week." He shrugged. "The house seemed too empty."

"They're a lot of responsibility."

"So I'm finding out." But he smiled. "He thinks my briefcase is a chew toy, and I have to get up half a dozen times at night to let him out, but I think I'm up to the challenge." He reached down to pat the dog. Then he asked, "Can you come in for a minute?"

"Sure." Julia expected the kids to protest after she said it. They were eager to get out trick-or-treating, so she added for their benefit, "But we can't stay long."

Apparently the chance to play with the puppy more than made up for the delay in their evening plans.

Danielle was already on her knees in the foyer, tiara askew, when she asked, "What's his name?"

"He doesn't have a name yet. Nothing seems to fit." Alec angled his head to one side. "Maybe you and Colin could help me come up with one."

"Sure!" Colin hollered over Danielle's more sedate, "I guess so."

They left the kids in the foyer. Alec charged them with passing out candy while they played with the puppy and came up with a name.

The great room looked different without the previous owners' big, comfy sectional taking up space. Alec's sleek leather couch had been a good fit for his apartment, but it was dwarfed here, the scale too small given the room's dimensions and high ceilings. He apparently read her mind.

"I need new furniture."

"Something a little larger," she agreed.

The dining room was empty. She followed him into the kitchen. She didn't recognize the canister set on the counter by the stove, or the assortment of copper-bottomed pots that was hanging from a rack over the island.

"These are new," she said.

"I'm taking some cooking lessons," he told her with a shrug. "I decided I didn't want to eat out for the rest of my life, especially now that I have a home."

"A dog *and* cooking lessons. Wow." She shook her head in amazement, not all of it teasing. Alec had done a lot of changing since she'd met him. Some of it to save his job. But this, in a way, was to save himself. Tears threatened. She blinked them back, and then her gaze caught on the plant she'd sent him. It was in front of the window, and most of its leaves were gone. Those that remained were edged in brown. He was probably overwatering it. Another plant was next to it, a larger one that was not in much better shape.

"Where did the palm tree come from?"

"The previous owners left it. Fred said he thought it was root bound. He said I should repot it. Maybe I need to take a class on plants, too." His smile was self-deprecating, endearing.

He was trying so hard to create a secure base for

himself. The sort of place he'd never known growing up. Feelings Julia had tried to deny bubbled back up.

"So, you're enjoying homeownership?" she asked.

"Trying." He stuffed his hands into the front pockets of his jeans and rocked back on his heels. Then he confessed quietly, "I almost put the house back on the market the week after I moved in."

"You did? Why?"

"I wanted a home and, well, it didn't feel much like one."

"I'm sure that was just because it was empty," she said.

From near the front door they heard the dog bark, followed by children's laughter.

This was what the house was missing, more so than furniture and window treatments. Alec's expression told her he knew that, even before he agreed, "It was empty. But it was missing more than furniture. It still is." He stepped closer. "How have you been?"

Heartsick. "Busy."

He lowered his voice. "I've missed seeing you. I've been tempted to say something stupid to a reporter again, just so we'd have to work together some more."

"Don't you dare!" She laughed. "I've been impressed with how well you've been doing on your own. The segment of you attempting to diaper a doll that aired on the local morning show last week was priceless. You're almost a natural when you're around kids now."

"It helped that it was a doll."

"Still. You showed patience, restraint and a good sense of humor."

"I guess I learned a few things from our time together." He reached over and gave her arm a squeeze.

The simple touch made Julia yearn. She swallowed around the lump in her throat. It struck her then, full force, not only how much she'd missed him, but also how much she had denied them both, how much she had denied her children, by bisecting her life in the short time they'd been together. Her sister had warned her. Julia hadn't listened. Not to her sister. Not to her own heart. Was it too late?

Shaken, she walked over to the plants. The palm tree probably had been lush in the beginning. What remained of its foliage now was stunted and dull. It stood nearly as tall as Julia, it's trunk as big around as her fist, but its roots were tucked into a pot no more than eight inches in diameter. The plant had long ago outgrown it.

As she studied it another leaf fell off and fluttered to the ground. Julia started to cry, not a mere misting of her eyes that she was able to control this time, but a vast waterfall of tears that washed down her cheeks. A sob escaped when Colin and Danielle's delighted laughter echoed from the foyer. She covered her face with her hands and wept.

Alec was beside her in an instant. "My God! Julia, what is it?" She felt his hands on her back, patting in comfort, but she wished that he would hold her.

"Fred's right. It's root bound. The pot is too small. It's too damned small," she managed to say after a minute. "This tree was beautiful once, but it's dying now. All because of the pot."

"Julia?"

She pulled her hands away. After a deep, bracing breath, she said, "I never told you I love you."

Alec had been patting her back, doing his damnedest to resist the urge to pull her into his arms and make a fool out of himself. Now his hand stilled and he forced her to turn and look at him.

"Can you say that again?" he said quietly, fiercely. "I want to be sure I didn't misunderstand.

"I love you." She smiled and his heart squeezed. Then she asked, "Is it too late to start over?"

"I don't want to start over," he told her honestly. He didn't want to go back. They'd come too far for that. He framed her face in his hands, caressing her cheeks with the pads of his thumbs. "I want to move forward, with you and the kids."

When he kissed her, Alec was home.

EPILOGUE

———

One year later...

      Alec stood at the altar and fought the urge to tug at his tie. Despite the church's air-conditioning, perspiration was beading on his forehead. Hurry up, already, he thought as he watched Julia walk up the aisle on her father's arm, her children on either side of them. A package deal, she'd once called it. A bargain, Alec thought now, though there had been bumps along the way. Plenty of them.

Julia smiled. She looked lovely in the fitted white suit, serene compared to his flurry of nerves. He took that as a good sign that she wasn't about to change her mind. They'd been engaged since Christmas and she'd initially wanted a year-long engagement, in part to give the children time to get used to the idea of their family of three expanding to four again. He'd talked Julia into eight months so that the kids would be settled in their new home before school started.

He couldn't wait until they were all under one roof,

starting a new life as a real family, the kind of family he'd never expected to have. He wasn't going to screw it up.

His gaze fell on his parents then. They were in the front pew overdressed for the understated occasion in designer clothes—the best that money could buy, of course. But at least they'd made it, or so Julia had reminded him when they'd jetted in late from a month-long sojourn in Belize. They were what they were, and they had no intention of changing. Just as Alec had no intention of ever being anything like them.

And so it was when Julia reached the altar and Lyle placed her hand in Alec's that he whispered fiercely, "I promise to be the best husband and father I can be."

The ceremony hadn't quite begun and the minister hadn't yet said anything about kisses, but Julia touched her lips to his.

"I already know that."

* * * * *

#9 THE SECRET WEDDING DRESS by Ally Blake

Paige Danforth isn't interested in setting herself up for an *un*happy-
ever-after—she knows the closest she'll ever get to walking down the
aisle is as a bridesmaid. But one bridal sale later Paige is left clutching
her dream wedding dress! Will commitment-phobic Gabe Hamilton
stick around when he discovers not only skeletons...but a lavish white
designer creation in her closet?

#10 DRIVING HER CRAZY by Amy Andrews

Journalist Sadie Bliss is on a mission to prove herself as a world-class
reporter. But when she embarks on a road trip across the Australian
Outback with dangerously mouthwatering photographer Kent Nelson,
she suddenly longs to throw her rule book out the car window. After
all, what happens in the Outback stays in the Outback...*right?*

#11 WHY RESIST A REBEL? by Leah Ashton

Ruby Bell has put scandal and relationships behind her to forge a
successful career in film. Then the talk of Hollywood himself, actor
Devlin Cooper, strolls onto her set after being fired from his past two
movies. He's looking decidedly devilish, but the last thing she needs is
Dev making outrageous demands...and proving that no one can resist
a bad boy....

#12 HER MAN IN MANHATTAN by Trish Wylie

It seems mayor's daughter Miranda Kravitz has scored herself a *very*
dreamy bodyguard! Apparently the fireworks between them are
scorching, but will this tabloid darling *really* be willing to give up her
newfound taste for freedom—no matter how gorgeous Tyler Brannigan
is? And will Tyler be able to keep this Manhattan princess in check
without resorting to the use of handcuffs...?

HKCNM0313

REQUEST YOUR FREE BOOKS!
2 FREE NOVELS PLUS 2 FREE GIFTS!

Trish Wylie brings you a contemporary story
of love, rebellion and trust with

HER MAN IN MANHATTAN

"I'm in your life now. Get used to it."

The flecks of gold that flared in her eyes hinted at a temper to match her hair. For a split second he wanted her to get mad enough to swing for him—to spit fire and passion and remind him of the woman he'd kissed.

As if sensing a weakness ripe for exploitation, she switched tactics. The curve of her full lips became sinful, drawing his gaze to her mouth and calling him to taste her again. She slowly ran the tip of her tongue over the surface, leaving a hypnotically glossy sheen in its wake.

In an instant he remembered how she'd felt when her body was melded to his, how soft her skin had been beneath his fingertips and how badly he'd burned for her. Just as suddenly he was aware of how close they were standing. One more step and their bodies would be touching again.

It took almost as much effort not to frown at his reaction as it did to snap his gaze back up to her eyes. "That won't work either, so you can forget it."

"I have no idea what you mean."

Sure she didn't. He reached for the door handle and jerked his chin. "Back up a step."

The battle of wills made the air between them crackle, and when her gaze briefly flickered to his mouth Tyler knew *that kiss* was as much on her mind as it had been on his. Her awareness of him was in the darkening of her eyes, in the increased rise and fall of her breasts. Any hope he'd had that what had happened between them could be blamed on the heat of the moment was gone. But while he'd lost his self-control once, he wasn't about to let it happen again.

"You getting in or am I putting you there?"

"You can't manhandle me like a common criminal," she replied on a note of outrage.

"Try me."

She glared at him as she took a step back. *"Door."*

Tyler held it open, unable to resist an incline of his head and a sweep of his arm in invitation. "Your highness…"

**Find out what happens next in
HER MAN IN MANHATTAN by Trish Wylie,
on sale March 19, 2013,
wherever Harlequin books are sold.**

HARLEQUIN

KISS™

Use this coupon to

SAVE $1.00

on the purchase of
ANY 2
Harlequin KISS books.

Available wherever books are sold, including most
bookstores, supermarkets, drugstores and discount stores.

✂ - - - - - - - - -

SAVE $1.00 ON THE PURCHASE OF **ANY TWO** HARLEQUIN KISS BOOKS.

Coupon expires July 31, 2013. Redeemable at participating retail outlets
in the U.S. and Canada only. Limit one coupon per customer.

52610686

CANADIAN RETAILERS: Harlequin Enterprises Limited will pay the face
value of this coupon plus 10.25¢ if submitted by customer for this product
only. Any other use constitutes fraud. Coupon is nonassignable. Void if
taxed, prohibited or restricted by law. Consumer must pay any govern-
ment taxes. Void if copied. Nielsen Clearing House ("NCH") customers
submit coupons and proof of sales to Harlequin Enterprises Limited,
P.O. Box 3000, Saint John, NB E2L 4L3, Canada. Non-NCH retailer—for
reimbursement submit coupons and proof of sales directly to Harlequin
Enterprises Limited, Retail Marketing Department, 225 Duncan Mill Rd.,
Don Mills, ON M3B 3K9, Canada.

5 65373 00033 5   (8100)1 18300

U.S. RETAILERS:
Harlequin Enterprises Limited will
pay the face value of this coupon
plus 8¢ if submitted by customer
for this product only. Any other
use constitutes fraud. Coupon is
nonassignable. Void if taxed,
prohibited or restricted by law.
Consumer must pay any govern-
ment taxes. Void if copied. For reimbursement submit coupons and proof
of sales directly to Harlequin Enterprises Limited, P.O. Box 880478, El Paso,
TX 88588-0478, U.S.A. Cash value 1/100 cents.

HKCOUP0213A

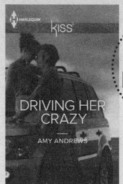